The Rings of Hubris

by

Carol Fortino

Cover Art

By

Ted Fusby

Order this book online at www.trafford.com
or email orders@trafford.com

Most Trafford titles are also available at major online book retailers.

Printed in Victoria, BC, Canada.

ISBN: 978-1-4251-8074-4

Our mission is to efficiently provide the world's finest, most comprehensive book publishing service, enabling every author to experience success. To find out how to publish your book, your way, and have it available worldwide, visit us online at www.trafford.com

Trafford rev. 3/31/10

www.trafford.com

North America & international
toll-free: 1 888 232 4444 (USA & Canada)
phone: 250 383 6864 • fax: 812 355 4082

To my mother,

A constant source of encouragement and love.

Acknowledgments

As a poet, switching to narrative necessitated changing succinct phrases into rich details. Many people helped me make this writing transition and special thanks goes to the following: my mother, Virginia Fortino, who noted scenes that needed embellishment; Marie-Laure Marecaux, my colleague from France who used her editing talents to keep the plot on track; English professor teacher, Dianne Brooks, who let not a comma nor dash go unnoticed; Sue Bassett, a careful critic and fine writer in her own right; Judy Fodor, my professional editor, and Judy Nemec for plot clarifications. Thanks once again to Ted Fusby, my long-time university friend, who created the cover art for this book.

"A man's character is his fate." Heraclites, c. 500 B.C.

FORWARD

Can we ever truly fathom how a killer's mind works? What convoluted thoughts impel someone to murder his loved ones, and, when necessary kill others, then seek exoneration through suicide? This story's beginning and end are purely fictional, imagined from gossip and hearsay. Names and places have been changed to protect the innocent. The plot was written many years before I was able to do any research into the facts that underpin the fiction. Details that resembled the truth were at first simply imaginary. In the end, I am not sure what unseen influences propelled me to create a story that so closely mimicked some of the bizarre realities.

St. George, Utah May 26, 2006

PROLOGUE

Hubris (hyoo´bris) – *Greek term for arrogance caused by too great pride.* Webster, 2000 A.D.

The passion of hubris may have served the gods well, but left unbridled, it condemned this man to evil actions. And yet, on the Ides of March, 1998, it was nature's sleight of hand that undid the hubris of the well-respected professor.

The month had been cooler than usual with occasional snow, rain, and popcorn hail peculiar to springtime. The early afternoon skies roiled with heavy clouds. The blackening billows were punctuated by lightning, signaling the beginning of the storm. Winds blew a soft drizzle of rain through the pines. Then larger droplets coalesced and splotched the ground. The thin soil was soon soaked and small puddles became rivulets, their contents sliding down the gently sloping hillside and into the creek bed. Gathering waters flowed from smaller tributaries charging the slow eddies into currents, washing around boulders, becoming brash and bold while assaulting the streambed. This storm front was unusual. It stalled and stayed stationary over the hills for several hours, then for two more days. This was an uncommon, but not an unrecorded event throughout the history of the dry Southwest.

The torrential rains continued to drench the foothills and swell the normally dry streambeds of the mesas. Objects began to move – soil, pebbles, gravel, rocks, boulders, tree trunks, old metal signs, fence posts, stranded cows. Scraggly piñons tenuously growing out of the layered sandstone were debarked. Chunks of the dry arroyo bed were debraided, uprooted, defaced and defiled. The gritty slurry crawled along the creekbed, scouring the banks while the brown, frothy water swirled up into the horizontal shelves, tearing out anything trapped in the sedimentary strata. Nothing was safe, not the hidden conglomerate rocks cemented in gypsum outcrops, not the stranded and bleached animal bones, not the whitened cow horns and antlers, not even human remains.

The water tore against the edge of the arroyo. An old, discolored cell phone splashed into the stream, crashed into a rock pile and was quickly buried under a boulder. A plastic mummy-like form dislodged from a limestone shelf. Held together with rotting duct-tape, it floated and swirled in the raging current, the plastic ripping as it bounced off rocks. It spun and snagged, twisted and cracked, making its way some twenty miles down the arroyo to settle at the bottom of a ravine where bones from the decomposed body would eventually be bleached white.

Forty-eight hours later the storm cell broke up and moved to the east. The resulting damage was immense. Water had spread through the adjacent short grass prairie, percolated through the thin layers of topsoil, leached into the subsoil, and then disappeared.

In just a few weeks, the seemingly devastating torrents would nurture a new cycle of spring growth. This flashflood would be recorded in the weather annals like the Thompson Canyon Flood of 1976 in the neighboring state of Colorado. Back then it took forensic scientists months to identify some of the victims whose faces had been peeled and sanded smooth by the slurry. They had used the newest holographic methods for plasticene face reconstruction, superimposing details from dental records to create human features of the flood's victims. Teeth and bits of their jewelry sometimes aided their identification.

However, in the Rio Seco Arroyo flood, little of value was lost besides a few cows that were stranded and drowned. That is, until later in the month. Two boys out exploring the mesa on their bikes found the bones of a decomposed partially clad human tangled in tattered strips of plastic.

PART ONE

Chapter 1

Highlands March 25th, 1998

Ring…ring…ring…ring.

Languidly, Sue Wilson stretched her long, slim body and fumbled for the phone across the cold metal rail of her hospital bed. She never understood why the doctor ordered drugs that depressed her when the vodka she mixed with orange juice tasted better and did the same thing.

"Hello," Sue answered groggily.

"Mrs. Wilson, this is Joe Thompson. You don't know me. I'm from Creekside. An article in the newspaper prompted me to call you. I found you in the phone book under Paul and Sue Wilson. When I called, a Mrs. Hines answered. She said she was your neighbor and was just there checking your house while you were in the hospital. I explained that I needed to talk to you right away, so she gave me the number to your room."

Sue forced herself to listen. She knew Kitty Hines wouldn't give out this number if the man hadn't sounded legitimate. No one had called her at the hospital, except Kitty, her mother and the kids. This man sounded serious.

"Mrs. Wilson, did you know that Professor Josh Blagsdale committed suicide two days ago?" Hearing only a slight intake of the woman's breath, Joe continued, "The newspaper implied that Paul Wilson may have been an accomplice in the death of Professor Blagsdale's wife. Professor Wilson is your husband, right?"

"What?...Paul?" Sue mumbled. She gathered her thoughts a moment, "Well, Josh and Paul were friends, but that was quite awhile ago. We divorced and Paul took a new position in New Jersey. He never even has time to come back to Highlands to visit his kids. What are you trying to tell me, Mr.?... What was your name, again? You have to forgive me, but I have been in the hospital for the last two weeks."

"Thompson, my name is Joe Thompson." Joe started his plea again, "Mrs. Wilson, my son, Ted Thompson, disappeared eight years ago on the same day that Rosa Blagsdale was reported missing. Her body – what's left of it – just washed out of Rio Seco Arroyo during the big flood last week."

"Rosa?" Sue thought as she stiffened her neck causing her gray-blonde hair to spread on the pillow around her long oval face. She gripped the phone more tightly. "Go on, Mr. Thompson."

"Two boys found Mrs. Blagsdale in one of the gullies out on the mesa. I mean the newspapers said that, according to the coroner's office, the identification was made through dental comparisons. Then the police reopened the missing person's case and all the evidence seemed to be pointing directly to her husband, the professor."

"What are you hinting at?" Sue countered. "They cleared Josh years ago of his wife's disappearance and the FBI briefly questioned my husband back then and found no connections. The authorities thought Rosa Blagsdale had been killed by one of those dangerous Mexican cartel families that she exposed in her novel about human trafficking. If I'm not mistaken, I think Josh took up a few years later with a Cheryl somebody."

"Mrs. Wilson, did you know that Cheryl Hornsby was found dead in Professor Blagsdale's garage six months ago? The police ruled it a suicide because her car engine was running and a hose was taped from the exhaust pipe to inside the front window. But now, after finding the professor's wife – I mean her remains – they think his girlfriend may have been murdered too."

"I am confused, Mr. Thompson. Why are you calling me?" Sue asked the stranger on the phone.

Joe paused and then said tentatively, "Mrs. Wilson, I am calling you because my wife has had this crazy idea for years that Professor Blagsdale had something to do with our son's disappearance. It's been eight years now, and we never found any clues for our Ted's disappearance. And the police, well, after the initial investigation, they just boxed up all the details of our son's disappearance as a cold case file."

“But with all this new evidence and now the professor’s suicide, even I am beginning to believe there might be something to my wife’s suspicions. Without your help, we might never find out if there was a connection to our son. Your husband's link to the professor might be our last hope. Please, is there anything you can think of?"

Sue seldom told anyone why she was in the hospital, only saying that her condition had flared up again. However, this seemed different. "Look Mr. Thompson, I am a recovering alcoholic. I'm in detox. No one believes what I say anyway."

"My wife will. You are her only shred of hope."

"I'll try to think about it for you. Leave me your number." As Sue hung up the phone, she began to drift into a medicinal haze, but her consciousness nudged her back to that day nine years ago in 1989.

She had just picked up her kids, Tommy and Amy, from school and dropped them off at their gymnastics class. She had an hour and a half to herself and decided to go home and have a quick drink before dinner. She drove into the driveway as usual and got out to pull open the garage door, a bit annoyed because Paul had promised to replace it with a new electric one before Christmas. As she pushed up the handle and started to lift, the whole door fell off its hinges, crashed down, and careened off her shoulder blade. With excruciating pain, she collapsed on the driveway. She hadn't even remembered the high-pitched scream that her neighbor Kitty Hines had heard. Kitty dialed 911 and then called Paul at the university. The secretary had to get Professor Wilson out of his late afternoon class. Sue woke up in the hospital that night with her dislocated shoulder in a sling and Paul told her that she had suffered a bad concussion.

Sue often thought, "I could have been killed. That door was fine when I closed it at 3:00 PM and I was only gone for 45 minutes. Did Paul suspect that I was going home to drink?"

He and Josh had gone camping the weekend before to Rio Seco Arroyo. Paul seldom explained what he and Josh talked about or what they did there. But since then, Paul had been in a querulous mood. They had argued about her increased drinking and the effect it was having on him and the kids. He shouted, "I am sick of your binges and if you don't do something about it, I will."

That old anger seared Sue's memory with embarrassment because she knew her addiction was the reason that no one believed the explanation about the unhinged garage door. When she had hinted her mistrust to the insurance adjuster, he had just concluded that metal fatigue and the cold weather would have contributed to the door's falling. Even her mother scoffed when she said, "I think Paul is trying to kill me!" But Sue was convinced that somehow Josh helped unhinge the door giving Paul an alibi since he was in class from 3:00 to 5:00. No one would even think to question the esteemed Professor Blagsdale.

Clearing her head of that ugly time, Sue tried to concentrate. "Now who are these Thompsons who called me? Why do they think I can help them, when I can't even help myself?" Sue rang for the nurse and for the first time since being admitted she asked to see the newspapers – all of them from last week.

Sue scanned the headlines, page after page, and finally found what she was after. A small headline on page three read: "College Professor Suspected of Murder Commits Suicide." The first paragraph zeroed in on the details. Professor Josh Blagsdale, a tenured professor of psychology and sociology at Mountain State

College committed suicide on March 25th. Police were investigating the alleged murder of his wife, Rosa Blagsdale, who had been missing for eight years and the death of his live-in partner, Cheryl Hornsby, six months ago. Bones and teeth of Mrs. Blagsdale were found by two boys in the Tenebrio Mesa area after the recent record-breaking flash flood, which scoured the left fork of the Rio Seco Arroyo ten miles east of Highway 35.

Sue looked at the file photo of Rosa. She recognized it as the photo from the dust cover of Rosa's book, *Lost and Recovered: The Tragedy of Human Trafficking*. There was her friend with the dark brown curls framing her roundish face. And those chocolate colored eyes, so penetrating and sparkling with intelligence - the beautiful, proud markings of Rosa's cultural heritage. Sue had quietly mourned her friend's disappearance all these years.

Sue read the article more carefully now. "Rio Seco Arroyo, that's where Paul and Josh used to go camping. How could there possibly be a connection to the Thompson boy?" she thought.

She lay back exhausted. For years, Sue hadn't concentrated on any details outside her yearning for a drink and where to find her hidden bottles. She barely had enough presence of mind to care for the children and make ends meet with the child support Paul diligently sent every month. Right now she just couldn't muster the energy to worry about someone else's nightmare. Yet when the nurse came in with her nightly shot, for once she refused.

As she began to relax, her thoughts began to filter through memories of the early years with Paul. There was a time when she had been a dazzling companion, a supportive academic wife, a good mother, even a community volunteer. After all, Sue Chenango had graduated summa cum laude as a political science major from UCLA. Not only her beauty but also her brains first attracted Paul Wilson, a budding Ph.D. historian, when they met on campus at an art opening of German war paintings. She had been interested in the social commentaries about the stolen art, while Paul was trying to put the Holocaust artists into an historical perspective. Their conversation led to a late night coffee and two years of steady dating. After finishing their degrees, they decided to marry, and it had seemed like a commitment to long-term happiness. Paul was excited to take a position as a new faculty member at Mountain State College.

It was hard to believe it was fifteen years ago that Paul met Josh Blagsdale while on some university committee. But that connection gave her the opportunity to become close friends with Rosa and her little boy, John. Sue remembered fondly how she and Rosa had shared together the excitement of their new pregnancies. Both delivered healthy baby girls, Rosa's little Julia and her own sweet Amy. When Tommy came along two years later, Rosa had been a godsend to Sue during that troubled pregnancy.

As the children grew, the families enjoyed joint backyard barbecues, especially on the Fourth of July, with Paul and Josh laughing and playing with the kids before setting off the fireworks. Sue remembered one 4th when the guys were getting ready to light the fireworks and she couldn't find the automatic flint. Josh pulled one out of his gym bag and said, off-handedly smiling at her, "You never know when you might have to hide the evidence." A bit taken aback by his wry sense of humor, Sue laughed and went to hustle the kids onto the porch. But, Josh's demeanor and the distant look in his eyes as he turned away made her a bit wary of their close friend.

Those were the early days filled with friends and young kids when Paul had still talked to her like the intelligent woman she was, or at least had been. They shared their dreams – hers about starting a career after the kids were raised and his about getting tenure and moving to a larger university. Once he confided in her about his boys-night-out when he and Josh went camping. It was the time they saw a total lunar eclipse during the Hunter's Moon. Josh loved astronomy and explained to Paul how the earth had passed directly between the sun and the moon, so that the only light hitting the full moon was from earth's own sunrises and sunsets, giving it Halloweenish red and orange hues. The men were awed and discussed one human being's insignificance in the grand scheme of the universe. They argued in an academic way about who or what is in control.

Those were cherished conversations with her husband before her vodka bottle became more important than her marriage. Sue wiped the tears that slid silently from her blue eyes over her high cheekbones and down her pale face. She thought a bit more about Josh recalling the summer nights when all the Blagsdale kids were sleeping in their beds and Amy and Tommy were snuggled under a quilt on the backyard porch swing. The couples would have a late night drink and philosophize. Josh revealed sarcasm not about people per se, but about life. He would quote Heraclites, "A man's character is his fate."

"What does that mean?" Rosa would argue.

Josh would explain, "If a man has too much pride in himself, he is doomed to his own fate." Rosa was as intelligent as her husband and staying home with three kids had not dulled that a bit. She was biding her time and Sue began to doubt that she had the same gumption.

As Sue finally began to doze off, she thought, "I never believed the story that Rosa was killed by some untraceable cartel mob. I knew her research was dangerous, but she would have confided those fears to me. And the vicious rumor that she had run off to Mexico to be with a lover. What was that supposed to hide? Our families had been too close and my friend had been as devoted a mother as I once was."

Rosa Blagsdale's unaccounted disappearance had been a shock to Josh's peers in the university community and it became a disappointment when the local, then the state police argued over jurisdictional turf. Then the FBI decided to involve the Mexican government through the International Bureau of Investigation. Two years later the investigation was shelved away as another cold case file involving international borders. No one had ever found a trace of Rosa – until now.

Sue slept fitfully, but suddenly she shot up in the dark with a searing memory stabbing her awake. Paul had once told her about something unusual that Josh and he had stumbled upon while camping. They were both amateur archeologists and loved to roam the arroyos to find pictographs and petroglyphs no one else had yet photographed. What had Paul told her? She searched her foggy memory urging herself to remember. Bits of sketchy information came back. They were looking for old Indian fire rings up on the bluff. While they were looking around, they discovered a deep shaft nearby. The shaft seemed unlikely in that old, metamorphic rock that formed the box canyon that drained into the sedimentary arroyo. They were puzzled as to why the deep hole had been dug out in the first place – this wasn't the right area for gold or silver mining exploration. Maybe it was a bore hole for an artesian well, they thought, since years ago there had been some talk of developing an old ranch homestead on that deserted acreage. They never figured it out.

Unaware of the late hour, Sue snapped on the light and dialed the Thompson's number. Although it was 2:30 AM, Joe answered the phone on the third ring. "Mr. Thompson," Sue hesitated, "maybe you should look for a mine shaft somewhere near the Rio Arroyo Seco campground. I really don't know anything else."

Joe's rough hands cradled the phone with a tender touch. He didn't know whether to wake up Nora and possibly fill her with false hope or to let her sleep the drugged slumber she had started the night of June 4th, 1990. No clues – that had been the worst of it for his wife. The Valium was a godsend that first week, but it made weeks blend into months, months into years. He couldn't wake Nora this morning until he knew something concrete.

Only Nora, grasping at improbable clues back then, had thought something was odd. Was it just coincidental that Ted had disappeared the same night that Professor Josh Blagsdale's wife Rosa had supposedly run off to Mexico or was killed by some professional cartel hit men? He never thought the two things had anything to do with each other, only that the Blagsdales had a summer cabin at Creekside. Joe recalled the annoying remarks Creekside's local Sheriff Gonzales made to Nora, "No needle was ever found in a proverbial haystack of random coincidences."

Joe decided to let Nora sleep as he quietly crept down the stairs. Maybe today he and the sheriff would find something for better or even for worse, something that he had feared for so many years. He started a pot of coffee and stared at the clock to count the hours before he could decently call Sheriff Mannie Gonzales. Sipping his coffee, Joe recalled the other early morning phone call years ago.

Chapter 2

The Arroyo March 26, 1998

Joe rang Sheriff Manuel Gonzales promptly at 7:00 A.M. “Mannie, this is Joe Thompson. I might have a lead about Ted.”

Sheriff Gonzales listened alertly. He had lived all his life in this part of New Mexico and was pleased to be assigned close to his hometown where he knew so many of the people. All these years he had been miffed about the Thompson case. Creekside was in his jurisdiction, even if the population was only 800. There had been only one murder in its history. A jealous husband shot the lover of an unfaithful wife, a cut and dried case since everyone knew the key players and no one was surprised. Nevertheless, the disappearance or murder of Joe's boy had been the nemesis of his career. If there were the slightest oddball lead, he would follow it.

Joe met Mannie at his office at 7:15. As he got into the police car, Joe said, "It only takes about forty minutes to drive out to the Rio Seco Arroyo campground. Do you know that area? I brought my section map just in case so I can navigate when we get closer." The two men rode in silence – nothing they could say could raise a balloon of hope because it could just as easily burst and disappear with a whoosh of despair.

As they drove down the interstate, Joe thought back to that day years ago when the sheriff questioned Ted's friends. No one had seen Ted except for his close buddy, Jim Vigil, who stopped by for gas at 6:30 P.M. that night on his way home from Highlands. The boys had talked about tomorrow's graduation ceremony but mostly about going to the party at Mary's house the next night.

Joe could still recall the details of the 8:15 AM phone call on graduation morning. He had thought that Ted had come home from work late and was in his bedroom upstairs sleeping in or getting ready for the big day. But he had not gone to check on him. Why would he? His tall, lanky son had been pretty independent since age 12, having odd jobs, being responsible for home chores, keeping his own bank account. He was the apple of his mom's eye, an only son and so handsome she would say. Ted had deep green eyes like his grandpa's. His body had a strong and sinewy frame that football practice toned. Joe and Nora were justly proud of having raised a great kid. Joe picked up the phone on the third ring.

"Mr. Thompson, this is Mary Hannigan. Ted is my graduation partner and he is not here yet. Could you please tell him to hurry up. Practice starts in fifteen minutes in the gym."

Joe called upstairs for Ted, but there was no answer. “Hold on, Mary,” Joe said, “He might be in the bathroom and can’t hear me. I’ll go check.” Joe went into his son’s room; either the bed had never been slept in or had recently been made up. It was obvious that Ted had not used the bathroom. "Mary, Ted's … not here right now."

"Well, where in the hell is he? Oh, I'm sorry, Mr. Thompson," Mary apologized.

"I don't know where he is," said Joe softly, with a dull blade of fear cutting into his belly.

The phrase, "I don't know where he is,” would echo hollowly for eight years while the police searched for his son. Did someone rob him during thc last few hours the gas station was open? But, Nora had called to remind him of something early in his shift, something about the graduation and he was fine then. Had he been working on a car up on the rack and didn't hear an intruder? Had somebody lured him into a car, a van? Nah, he was too smart and athletic for that.

A few weeks earlier his son had shared his excitement about already having been accepted to Mountain State in Highlands. Ted was ranked second in his class and was supposed to be – no, IS the salutatorian of his class. He said he wanted to be a mechanical engineer with a psychology minor. Joe and Nora wondered to themselves who had planted that silly combination of ideas in his head?

Joe dragged his attention back to the present as Sheriff Gonzales stopped the four-wheel drive police Bronco at the primitive Rio Seco Arroyo campground. There were no water or toilet facilities available, so the rangers rarely checked it. The two men could tell that no one had been at the campground for a long time.
The men got out of the vehicle and started down the left fork of the arroyo, amazed at the devastation from the flash flood. Normally the layers of sedimentary rock lay undisturbed in the semi-arid

desert. Seeping rainwater and occasional floods hollowed out ragged horizontal crevices in the shale and limestone, evidence of the old Cretaceous Sea that once inundated the Southwest. Sheriff Gonzales kicked some broken gastropod and brachiopod fossils protruding from their limestone matrices. Joe bent down for a closer look at a small round ammonite that lay in the rubble with some of its pearly nacre shining in the strong sunlight -- ancient life forms washed away from their quiet graves. From here there was no evidence of the hand-painted pictographs and petroglyphs stippled by the Anazazi onto large flat slabs of rock indicating a haunting human presence. The creekbed was dry and dusty as usual, all signs of the ravaging flood from two weeks ago had been obliterated by the relentless desert sun.

"Sue Wilson said to look for a mineshaft," Joe said quietly to the Sheriff. "I think we might find it up on the mesa and not down here in the arroyo." The two men scrambled up a makeshift path to get to the top of the mesa five feet above the sandy creekbed. They spread out and began to examine the land populated mostly with yucca, cholla, ocotillo and an occasional mesquite tree. Prickly pear and four-wing rabbit brush dotted the landscape while in the distancc a mountain mahogany bush grew. Not a likely site for a mineshaft or well bore, they thought as they walked slowly for about two hundred yards and found nothing. They started again at slightly different angles. The sun was getting stronger and they hadn't brought much water.

"Maybe we should come back with more folks," the beer-bellied sheriff suggested.

"Just a while longer, Mannie. Let's try one more path. You take the north side, I'll take the south." The men bent low as they walked slowly looking for any signs of disturbance.

"Hey, Joe," Mannie called out. "There is a large piece of old board here. Give me a hand." Joe walked over and looked at the flat, rotted piece of wood. Together they shoved it to the left and then lifted the edges. Underneath was a four-foot diameter hole. They peered in and saw only darkness. Mannie picked up a small rock and tossed it in. It took a few seconds for them to hear the dull thud at the bottom of the shaft. The men looked at each other n anticipation. "Let me go back to the car and get my flashlight," the sheriff said.

Joe stood there looking out across the short grass prairie. He could feel no emotion, as if he were in suspended animation. He wouldn't let his mind project what they might find. Mannie returned sweating heavily and breathing like someone who has spent too much time smoking and riding around in his Bronco. The men got down on their knees and directed the light into the deep shaft. "I don't see any water. Wait, there is a lump of some kind."

“Joe, we need to get some help out here.” Mannie returned to the cruiser and radioed into town forty miles away. Highlands was a town of sixty thousand and had a full police force.

"Detective Hidalgo, this is Sheriff Manuel Gonzales. I may have found a body and need your help." Mannie gave directions to Rio Seco Arroyo campground and Hidalgo said he would get his people out there within the hour. The two men made their way back to the SUV and sat in silence, waiting.

A city rescue vehicle made its way slowly down the bumpy, pot-holed road to the campground. Sheriff Gonzales explained the situation and two men set out toward the open shaft. Bill Fendel was harnessed and lowered down by ropes.

"It's dark down here, but there is only a little water seepage on the sides. It doesn't have the smell of well water. Too shaley to have valuable ores – not sure what this fifty foot hole was for, but it makes a good hiding place."

"Cut the chatter," Bill heard in his headphones, "I've got the speaker on and Mr. Thompson is a civilian up here."

The rescue worker let his feet touch the wet muck while his helmet torch illuminated the side walls. He aimed his flashlight around the bottom of the shaft. Then he saw them – a pile of bones. He could identify a femur, tibia and fibula. The small ankle bones were scattered about. The cranium and one humerus lay akimbo. Either this person died in the fall or was dead when he or she was dropped down the well. The phalanges of the right hand had disarticulated from the wrist bone and lay at a forty-five degree angle from the ulna and radius. The muscles and tendons had long since rotted away, but the bones were not bleached white as they might have been in strong sunlight up above. "Where was the right arm and leg? The body must have landed on that side," thought Fendel. It reminded him of pictures of the stretched out arm of the 5000 year-old Ice Man found in Italy.

He then took photos of everything in situ. When he nudged the scapula aside, Fendel saw some scattered vertebrae and finger bones under the ribs. A glint of blue caught his eye. He loosened the harness, not knowing how firm the ground was underneath him, and bent down to retrieve the metal object. The flashlight let him read the words, "Creekside High School, Class of 1990." He put the ring in a plastic bag and began to place the bones in the net bag. Normally he would tug the line and let his partner lift the bag out first. Today he knew it could be the father of the missing boy waiting up above.

PART TWO

Chapter 3

Juanita 1966-68

The northern coast of Venezuela was beautiful with its deep blue hues of the Caribbean ocean. Josh Blasgdale looked out across Cata Bajon and the Point, jutting out a half mile from the coast and forming the right arm of the bay. The sheer white cliff-face was darkened on top by coastal shrubs. The Henry Pittier National Park was not far from Caracas and showcased the flora and fauna of the region. For bird watchers or beach lovers this was a special place. The waves were running at 3-4 feet, making a booming concatenation as they combed along the beach. Only a few *Caraqueños* from the city were around this Tuesday.

It was August 1965, as Josh lay back on the white sandy beach. Long lanky legs extending from his bikini swim trunks were beginning to tan. His auburn hair was slightly bleached and helped offset his blue eyes. He felt proud of his six foot two, one hundred-eighty pound physique. He smiled as he remembered the girl he dated as an undergrad who had nicknamed him "my Adonis." The self-pride in his physique was out-done only by a self-indulged narcissism for his own mental prowess. Josh always credited this trait to his father, who abandoned the family when he was eight, leaving his mother to nourish his sense of self-worth.

He had lucked out getting this three-year post-grad fellowship in psychology. When he wasn’t studying the children who lived in the *favelas,* the cardboard shanties on the hills of Caracas, he was at the beach or in the jungle near the city. The head of his department was cool and didn't expect him to be in the office every day. The pretext for today's beach apathy was that he was writing up field notes from last week's interviews of the teenagers who survived the high poverty and frequent crime rate in the city and ranchos. In any case, Josh had brought along one of his research books and some documents written by the Baptist missionaries who worked in the *barrios*. That should count for quasi work. “Funny,” he thought, “how we inland types have to legitimize excuses for enjoying time at the beach. Who says you can't work efficiently with thc sound of surf as a background?”

After taking a quick dip, Josh gathered his books and beach towel and headed to the juice shack, a bamboo stand whose specialties were the local coconut and barley drinks. While counting out his pesos, he noticed a beautiful tall, slim girl – no, a young woman about twenty. She had picked up her drink and was walking away. Boldly, Josh used his ever-improving Spanish, "*Buenos dias, señorita*," he said. She eyed him coolly and nodded. Her stately frame and olive face looked familiar, and he remembered that he had seen her around the university, but not in his department. He introduced himself and asked her name, mentioning that he had seen her on campus. She smiled slightly by way of reply. He asked if they might sit together while they sipped their *horchatas,* tiger nut milk. Josh chuckled at the thought of such a pleasant tasting drink masked by such a fierce name.

Josh's listening skills were better than his speaking fluency. But he nevertheless attempted to use his ever improving Spanish. "*Yo soy Josh Blagsdale, y usted*?" He found out that Juanita Flores was a graduate student in English and worked part-time as a teaching assistant. Her dark eyes mesmerized Josh as she spoke. Noting his halting Spanish, Juanita switched to quite fluent English. He told her about finishing his Ph.D. at Berkeley in May

'65 and how this post doc research might give him the niche of expertise he would need to eventually land a tenure-track job in his field of psychology.

Juanita replied, "I understand the pressures of academia because my papa is head of the Mathematics Department." Juanita rose, gracefully brushing back her long black hair and said she had to return for her late afternoon class. Josh, brazen in his American way, asked for her phone number, then smiled and asked if he might call her.

After an intense courtship, Josh and Juanita were married later that year in the local Catholic Church. Her father, Dr. Alfonso Flores, and her mother, Marita, walked her down the aisle, as was the custom. Several of her cousins draped a large wooden rosary around the bride and groom who pledged to be committed to God, the Church and each other until death would part them.

Juanita and Josh began a tradition that for each anniversary they would plan something special. The first year Josh surprised Juanita with a day trip to Curaçao to see the beautiful Dutch buildings in Willemstad near Breedestraat dating from the 1600s. Then they went snorkeling, enjoyed a wonderful dinner and stayed at a little hotel he had read about.

While snorkeling, the couple floated slowly hand-in-hand enjoying the mounds of star coral that resembled massive mushrooms. Then they knelt quietly on the shallow white sandy bottom watching the colorful fish. Near Juanita's right arm a fierce-looking moray eel suddenly poked its head out of the rocks. That was enough to spook her, and they headed back to the beach.

While waiting for their food at the seaside restaurant, Josh read Juanita the notes on the back of the colorful menu. It described the territorial tongue called Papiamento, a mix of languages that allowed the early traders from various countries to communicate with one another. He read her one example, "Pampuna no sa pair calbas" – the pumpkin vine does not bear calabash."

"What do you think that means?" Juanita asked Josh.

He thought for a minute and said, "The fruit doesn't fall far from the tree – like father, like son." They were laughing at Josh's odd translation when their food arrived.

During the next year, Josh continued sending out resumes for a full-time position, as he had done since before arriving in Venezuela. At that time he wasn't married and had always filled in single on his applications. Two offers had come through, and Josh flew back to the USA alone for the interviews. Then in May, a firm offer from Brandon University arrived, and Josh flew back to Nebraska for the interview. With his fellowship ending next year, he began to process papers for Juanita's green card.

It was a nightmare. With the Vietnam War still being waged, immigration rules had been tightened, even for those married to Americans, because of the tremendous influx of immigrants trying to get into the country. "Green-tape" translated into money, letters of application, and waiting, endless waiting. It was turning out to be more entangled than red-tape. He was coming to the harsh realization that if he were going to pursue his academic dreams back home, this marriage would need to end. But that left him with a dilemma because for once his pride had been tempered by love for his beautiful, intelligent wife. His animal sense of survival, however, began to override his emotions of loyalty. He began to plot a way out. But he would have to be patient a while longer.

For their second anniversary Juanita planned a horse-back trip into the jungle where they floated down some wonderful fresh streams, ate ripe bananas hacked from the trees, and stayed at a lovely hacienda.

The next year it was Josh's turn, and he planned a trip to Augustina Falls, a four-hour drive from Caracas. The day was hot and steamy as they drove along the northern coast passing through the Sabana de Mayupa plains. They took a short detour to stop at the Arautaima Rapids and to throw a coin into the Pozo de la Felicidad, the Fountain of Happiness. Then they continued on, turning inland heading to a series of waterfalls that descended the face of the Auyanatepuy Mesa. The last ten miles wound through the jungle entwined with liana and strangler figs and up to a rocky escarpment. Another mile of rough road along the ledge led to a beautiful vista point above the falls. The water made a narrow, white misty bridal veil in contrast to the verdant valley spread around it. The spray was refreshing as they walked carefully near the edge looking down on the Carrao River.

"Shall I get the picnic basket?" Juanita asked, pressing Josh's hand warmly as they looked at the breathtaking view.

"Not just yet. Let's just enjoy the view for a few more minutes."

Josh's arms encircled Juanita's waist. "I do love you, *mia cara*," Josh murmured in her ear. She looked into his eyes and kissed him tenderly. He gently spun her outward, pointing to the arc of the rainbow created by the mist of the falls. Josh slowly moved his left arm and pulled a flat stone from his pocket. He carefully aimed a single blow to the back of her head. Stunned, Juanita began to slump forward, but Josh turned her around to face him one more time and nudged her limp body over the edge.

A quiet Venezuelan rain chant hummed in his mind as Josh drove carefully down to the main road where he telephoned for an ambulance from Caracas. It was late afternoon by the time the local *policia* arrived to retrieve Juanita's body from the rocky sandbar at the bottom of the falls. They concluded it was an accidental fall from the slippery rocks above since the back of the woman's head had been crushed when she landed, and one of her stiletto shoes had washed down the river. Josh never had understood why South American women insisted on wearing those treacherous high heels, but today that cultural affectation had served his purpose well.

Professor Alfonso Flores was waiting with his distraught wife when the ambulance arrived. The siren was silent. The local coroner declared the death of their daughter accidental due to the slippery rocks and the steep ledge. Before the body was covered, Josh asked his father-in-law if he might take off Juanita's wedding ring as a remembrance of his love for her. Overcome by the sudden loss of his only daughter, the distraught father nodded his approval and Josh slid the inscribed ring into his pocket.

The funeral was well attended by the colleagues of Professor Flores, the many friends of Juanita, and a few people from Josh's department. As the weeks crawled by, Josh settled into the sullen posture of a young widower and his colleagues left him alone with his grief. Then a month later, the promised position from Brandon University came through. Josh said his good-byes and left Venezuela.

As the plane took off, Josh relaxed in his seat and looked back at the high Venezuelan peaks surrounded by fog. He closed his eyes and thought of Juanita. His tall wife with her coppery skin would have made a beautiful life's companion had immigration snarls not interfered. He took out his favorite photo, signed “From your loving wife! Juanita, Caracas, 1968" and placed it between the pages of his leather-bound journal. Her wedding ring was already hidden in the statue of the UC Berkeley campanile that would sit on his new office desk. He reasoned soundly that no one really needed to know about this marriage. He had indicated single on all his applications, which was truthful at the time, and he had never mentioned his subsequent marriage in his interviews. He did not leave a forwarding address with Professor Flores, instead saying he would write when he was settled. The fact of Juanita would be buried in the small Caracan cemetery.

PART THREE

Chapter 4

Rosa 1969-77

Brandon University was situated in the small town of Essex, population about 70,000. The town doted on its college atmosphere that enhanced community activities and, occasionally, stirred up local politics. The tree-lined avenues and old stone buildings gave the place a scholarly feel, although nothing like Josh's fond memories of Sather Gate and the UC Campanile he had so loved while studying at Berkeley. The campus did at least boast of a new coffee house, Iggie's. It would do for now until he found out more about the area.

Josh was soon occupied getting settled into his two-bedroom apartment that was near enough to campus so that he could ride his bike and keep in shape. He worked diligently on writing the course syllabi for the fall semester: two large lecture classes of Psychology 101 and one new graduate seminar for M.A.

students in his department. The university had recently started an interdisciplinary humanities program that culminated in two-semesters of senior seminars. Josh was excited to be part of this innovative team-taught course.

The twenty students came from several disciplines: English, foreign language, science, and psychology. The new course presented broad themes, such as the economics of war and the psychology of survival. Lively debate ensued as students argued from their own areas of expertise, honed by four years of study. It was a heady atmosphere that began to rival some of his own seminars at Berkeley, but this time, he noted with carefully masked pride, he was the professor.

The first semester went by smoothly and Josh made a few friends in his department. His teaching evaluations were good and his department chair was happy with the new faculty member. Josh occasionally churned out another paper on the life-coping strategies of the *huelepega*, the abandoned children whom fate had deposited in the poverty-ridden *favelas* of Venezuela. His terse academic style described the turf wars that raged among the rival gangs trying to dominate the *favelas* for their drug markets and the killings that marred the daily lives of the children. One article, accepted to a peer-reviewed journal, described the government's proposals to stop the urban violence that was spiraling out of control. Children bartered their young lives running drugs since they could earn five to ten times the minimum wage.

Josh's research was based on the fact that inside the *favelas* there was little opportunity for employment for the uneducated. One government scheme he uncovered attempted to secure the cooperation of the local drug lords. It allowed a non-profit group, *La Gente,* to set up special programs for boys between the ages of 15 and 20. If the boys earned a certificate, they could go to work in Caracas. The ulterior motive of the drug lords was to pare down the growing pool of young men joining rival gangs in the *favelas*. Only a few of the smartest boys would be recruited into the inner circle of the cartel. Josh discussed this idea with his colleague, Professor Gordon, saying, "This NGO scheme at least empowers the boys to have a personal sense of survival."

The professor countered Josh's premise arguing, "It is a cynical and calculated approach! What if that was the only option for American ghetto kids?"

"Some of them don't even have that choice," Josh said authoritatively. "Listen to this other government idea. The Venezuelans want to help stem the crime in the *favelas,* so they suggest building a wall around the perimeter of area and using police checkpoints for entry and exit. I think this one is a hair-brained idea. It would simply turn the impoverished shantytowns I've seen into living cemeteries. Besides, their soldiers are not trained for urban conflict, and that's what it would lead to because the drug lords won't let anyone dictate terms for them."

Professor Gordon responded soberly, "These ideas only show the desperation of the Venezuelan government. They certainly are not feasible solutions, except maybe the educational one. Not that the US has any better ideas in the hopper."

Josh was able to publish a few articles in peer-reviewed journals, a necessary requirement that would signal his academic career was going well. He prided himself on foreseeing that his specialized area of research could become the niche of expertise that would provide entrée into his close-knit academic field of psychology. He understood that academia was a field that necessitated extreme pride in onesclf, almost to the point of arrogance.

In his quiet moments, Josh felt lonely and missed the intimate companionship he had shared with Juanita, although he seldom allowed thoughts of her to enter his mind. His narcissism made him realize that to really join the serious academic ranks, he would need another wife.

During one of his sessions he taught for the senior seminar, Josh noticed one dark-haired, lively girl named Rosa Munoz who had a slight trace of an accent. As the group introduced themselves, the girl mentioned that she was from Mexico and was taking her undergraduate studies at Brandon to help improve her English. He could tell she was from aristocratic Spanish-Mexican heritage with the fine facial features and long slender hands that marked her as a classic beauty even though she stood only five feet four. As an English major, Ms. Munoz's background in literary criticism trained her to be an astute analyst of the arguments presented in the seminar. She had a rather legalistic mind, and he wondered if she planned to be a lawyer. Each time he saw her, he was as intrigued by her body as he was by her intellect. But, he knew better than to cross the relationship line between professor and student while teaching the class. Not that this kind of infringement didn't happen on campuses everywhere, but he was not willing to jeopardize his future academic goals. Putting his emotions on hold, he reasoned that perhaps he would pursue this romantic interest in the spring.

Spring semester began uneventfully, but Josh kept a lookout for Rosa Munoz. Then one day he saw her at the student union and invited her to eat lunch at his table. She was a bit surprised, but in all honesty, she too had noticed the professor with more than a scholarly interest last semester. It now seemed appropriate to take him up on the simple sharing of a table.

As he listened, Josh was able to flesh out details about Rosa's background. He learned that she was from a wealthy family in Guadalajara who had a summer home on Lake Chapala. Her eyes lit up when she told him about learning to water ski at age fourteen. Her favorite place now was the area around Lake Pátzcuaro. She was surprised that Josh had never visited her country, given his academic interest in peasants locked in poverty. She wanted to be a political writer someday and analyze the serious emigration and financial problems of her country. Rosa revealed a sense of social consciousness not always found in upperclass Mexican society. She thought that studying law at some future time and earning a J.D. would be a reasonable pathway to help her untangle her country's legal problems. She had learned in her political science class about the Bracero program that ran from 1942 through 1964, allowing Mexican nationals to take temporary farm work in the United States. As predicted, the government decision to halt the program simply led to more and more illegal immigrants trying to get across the Mexican border. Surely the governments of both countries would have to work cooperatively on this growing problem, and she wanted to be part of the solution.

As Rosa talked, Josh took more detailed notice of her petite figure and beautiful complexion, her dark wavy hair setting off deep chocolate eyes. He contemplated asking her for a date, but for now they just said a friendly goodbye. The time would come, he thought. At least he knew more of her schedule and could arrange to run into her more frequently. Two weeks later he saw her again and they ate with a group of profs and students from last semester's seminar. By the end of the month, he figured he could safely ask her for a date, and she accepted.

Josh and Rosa "courted," an old-fashioned word that fitted her upbringing as a girl of high-class Mexican status. At least, they weren't accompanied by a *dueña* on their dates. They saw movies and ate out regularly and it was generally known that they were seeing each other. Then he asked her to go away with him one weekend to a small cabin. Instead of shying away, Rosa accepted. That was the beginning of their committed relationship.

Teaching summer sessions typically fell to junior faculty – a cheap way to boost their minimal salaries. It worked well because Rosa had to finish two courses during summer school. By August, Josh had asked Rosa to marry him. They flew to Mexico to meet her family before the fall term. Rosa’s parents were duly impressed with her choice of a promising young professor who spoke Spanish, although with a South American accent, and the Muniz family gave their blessing for a winter wedding.

During the Christmas break, Josh and Rosa were married in the Guadalupe Cathedral right off the Plaza near the Museo Regionale. Rosa made a beautiful bride wearing the old-fashioned silk gown that her mother had worn, delighting the elderly dignitaries of Guadalajara who were in attendance. Through her father’s political influence, the reception was held in the Palacio de Gobierno. All the extended family, including her favorite aunt, enjoyed the day of celebration, watching the tall blond man with the blue eyes dance with their beautiful Rosa, holding her securely.

For their honeymoon the newlyweds traveled to Pátzcuaro, the former capital of the old Tarascan Indian kingdom. The small town rose above the shores of the beautiful azure lake. It was like an artist's canvas with its small, nestled villages and unusual fishing boats, the hallmark of the area. Typical cobble-stoned streets surrounded the small plazas and old churches. The houses were limed, stark white, with red tile roofs.

Josh and Rosa stayed at the Hotel Mansión Iturge Lago, the one suggested and paid for by Señor Munoz. The décor with its heavy wood furniture and lace curtains gave it an ambience of colonial times with a corner fireplace that kept the foyer warm in the wintery chill.

The next day the newlyweds visited the *mercado* near Plaza Grande and bought a piece of Indian lacquer-ware for their small apartment in Brandon. The couple took the *colectivo* boat to Janitzio, the island famous for its ancient Aztec celebration of Dia de los Muertos, and hiked up to the statue of the patriot Morelos to look out over the views of Lake Pátzcuaro.

They felt a contentment that seemed to bode well for their future happiness. Josh never once thought about his previous love. But in the depths of his psyche, he knew that this marriage to Rosa, even though it would be filled with passion, would also be one of convenience – a rung on the ladder for attaining his personal, academic goals.

When they arrived back home, the couple enjoyed decorating their small apartment with wedding gifts they had brought back in two extra suitcases. The spring semester found them inseparable, enjoying one another's company and hosting small dinner parties. Rosa continued studying for her finals, while Josh was busy grading essay papers. It was in early May that Rosa told Josh she was pregnant.

Chapter 5

Mountain State College 1978-1989

In early June, Josh got a tenure-track offer from Mountain Sate College in southern New Mexico with a $10,000 increase in salary. This new job would help pay for their first baby, and he reasoned that this liberal arts college was a step up from Brandon. In the long run, the position was a necessary springboard for furthering his career at a larger university.

It was late afternoon when Josh and Rosa drove toward the town of Highlands, coming down the steep pass between canyon walls of Caballo Mountains. The Rio Grande River snaked a slow green pathway alongside the highway. A wall of horizontal red-banded sandstone rose up on one side contrasting with the bent syncline of grey granite with quartz intrusions on the opposite side. As they neared the outskirts of the town, flat-topped mesas stood out in the blue haze of the horizon and the shadowed side canyon arroyos showed deep furrows and horizontal washouts from occasional flash floods known to ravish this arid New Mexican landscape.

They drove through the center of town, pleased to see that it was large enough to support a fairly large shopping mall. They kept their eyes out for a local Mexican restaurant, not the chain outfits they saw on the Mall's marquee. Rosa spotted the Cantina where they could eat later after unpacking a few boxes.

They drove farther along to the Mountain State campus. The entrance was landscaped with an artificial oasis of green. A Spanish-style fountain splashed into a large round basin, making a stark but pleasant contrast to the arid land they had just driven through. They checked the map to find the cul-de-sac with their designated faculty house. It wasn't as bad as they had expected – a Spanish-style adobe ranch house typical of the area. Someone had even kept the small patch of lawn watered, although a variety of cacti was the main feature of the yard.

Josh quickly settled in as the fall semester began, staying busy with new classes. To become part of the faculty team, he got himself appointed to several committees. At one long, drawn-out meeting he sat next to another new faculty member, Paul Wilson from History. They met for coffee afterwards and found that they were both married, new to the area and, in the course of conversation, they discovered that they both had a burgeoning interest in amateur archeology. They planned a trip during the upcoming Christmas break to a nearby site that contained a noted canyon wall featuring six-fingered hands and fetish pictographs plus a few archeo-petroglyphs with stippled forms of animals and hunters.

Shortly into the new year, Rosa gave birth to the son they christened John. Josh proved to be an attentive father. Sensing Rosa's need for a network of friends, he introduced her to Paul's wife, Sue, and the women became close friends. Sue, who doted on baby John, was eager to have a child of her own.

Two years seemed to pass rather quickly for the two friends with kids, faculty wives club, and couples dinners. Sue Wilson even had time to audit a class on art of the Southwest. She particularly enjoyed giving Rosa a break some afternoons as she watched Johnny Blagsdale grow, toddle, then walk. He was a happy but serious little guy. The big blue eyes that he had inherited from his dad always seemed to be watching and understanding, although he was rather late talking in clear phrases.

Sue was ecstatic when both she and Rosa found they were pregnant at the same time. They shared the ups and downs of the next nine months, getting through morning sickness, eating lots of ice cream, and preparing for the births. Julia Blagsdale and Amy Wilson were born only a few days apart and their mothers had fun treating them almost like twins.

While the new mothers were busy, the guys took off several weekends to go to their favorite camping spot. They always brought home some artifact they had found, spending hours researching it at the University. The librarian, Vicki Bernstein, was really helpful since petroglyphs of the Southwest had been one of her major study areas and she loved this excuse to delve into something different from her normal work.

When the couples had a neighborhood get-together, Sue loved to watch Josh and Rosa together as it was obvious that Josh adored his wife. Josh got a kick out of being the barbecue chef and always wore a tall white hat and the plastic Disneyland apron his kids had bought him for his birthday. Josh was a good storyteller, a trait he had developed in order to keep his large audiences of freshmen interested in their introductory course. Josh regaled his dinner companions with a new story. "The other day I told my class how Professor Wilson almost stepped on a canyon rattler while prying out an old arrowhead." Josh chortled, "I said that he seemed to teleport across the pathway and I wasn't sure how he got that far away. I demonstrated jumping in front of the podium pretending the microphone cord was a snake. Like magic, eh!" Paul gave a chuckle and smiled at his friend. Yet the spontaneity of his friend in this setting was contrasted by a more brooding personality that Paul noted during their camping trips.

When the kids all fell asleep in front of the TV and the grown-ups were left talking over one last drink by the barbecue, Sue Wilson also glimpsed a more sinister side of Josh. Something she couldn't quite put her finger on and nothing she would ever hint to Paul or Rosa. Maybe it was just that academic arrogance, a common veneer among university professors. But Josh seemed...What? More cunning? Josh had a ruthlessness her sweet Paul never did possess, especially when their friend was describing someone at the university whose intellect he didn't particularly respect.

Sue's vague concern about Josh vanished when both families increased in size, each with one last child, the Blagsdale's Joanie and her own little Tommy. Her pregnancy with Tommy had been a rough one and Rosa, the supermom, was a godsend through it all. Paul Wilson admired Josh. Although Josh was not much older, in a sense he became Paul's mentor. Paul knew that Josh would become chair of the psychology department one day in the pedantic order of all things academic. At the same time, Josh was one of the few men that Paul considered a close friend.

During camping trips, they discussed their work and families. One night when the campfire was almost out, Paul revealed a rare anger. "Sue has been drinking more and more, and it's driving me crazy. Sometimes we meet for happy hour at the faculty club on Friday afternoon and she can almost drink me under the table. At home she used to ask if I wanted a drink before dinner, but not long ago, I found her with a glass of booze in her hand when I came in the door. She didn't even ask if I wanted to join her. I'm getting tired of this. The worst is, I found an almost-empty bottle under the bed when I went to get my slippers. Oh, she made excuses, first about continuing post-partum depression after Tommy and now menstrual cramps. Paul sighed, "My patience is just wearing thin and I worry about the kids. They might be better off without her."

Josh sat in silence and then, staring at the dying fire, said slowly, "If you're that disgusted, I might have an idea of how to solve the problem permanently." Paul listened, intrigued by his friend's plan. But it was so drastic, that he would have to think long and hard about it. Putting the fire out, the two men went to their separate tents.

At one point, Sue Wilson was hospitalized after tripping on Amy's bike in the back yard, a simple home accident it was reported. No one but her mother and Rosa knew that she went away after that to an alcoholic recovery spa. At the hospital Pat Chenango pleaded with her daughter, "I just don't understand why you do this, Sue! Paul loves you and is so worried about you. Amy and Tommy need you at your best." But no amount of coercion from her husband, mother or her good friend Rosa would help Sue regain her previous sense of purpose.

So the doctor suggested an intervention meeting with Sue and her support system. At the meeting, he said, "All of you have to quit being Sue's co-dependents." Looking directly at Sue, he continued, "You will either hit bottom, lose your family, and perhaps die, or you can decide your family is worth the fight back. It won't be easy."

When Rosa finally told Josh about her friend's dilemma, he wasn't as sympathetic as she thought he would be. Josh only remarked bluntly, "Let her stew in her own juices."

The next year Paul was offered a better job out of state, and eventually the Wilsons divorced, leaving Sue with only enough financial support to manage the two children as best she could. She made an effort to pull herself out of the vortex of continual alcohol cravings, but she was often sucked back in. Luckily, her mother would come to help her when she went to the hospital for detox.

Although Sue and Rosa remained friends, Rosa began to rely more on her next-door neighbor, Nina Schultz, who had a daughter Julia's age. They shared driving the girls to ballet classes while John rode his bike to soccer practice and Joanie played at home with the neighborhood babysitter. Maybe now, Rosa hoped, she would have some time to pursue her own writing dreams - dreams she had had since her heady Brandon University days, before her demanding academic marriage and the care of young kids forced her to put them on hold. It was time for her now.

Chapter 6

Lost and Recovered

Rosa had first toyed with the idea of writing a children's book, embellishing some mystical tales from her Mexican childhood. She read the drafts aloud to John and Julia, but being American-culture kids, they didn't particularly like the stories. So she began searching through her undergraduate children's literature books for ideas and decided her kids were old enough to enjoy Lewis Carroll's *Alice in Wonderland.* John, now 8 and a precocious reader, loved the sounds and nonsense words of the book's poem "Jabberwocky." Showing off his excellent memory, John would recite much of it by heart and teased his sisters saying it was a "brillig" day and they were only little "mimsy borogroves." Rosa tried combinations of children's tales, but she finally realized that this genre of writing just didn't have the substance she was seeking for herself.

One day in the fall Rosa received a letter from her aunt in Guadalajara telling her about a neighbor's daughter who had gone missing from the town's plaza. The young teenager, Marcellina Padilla, had been kidnapped, taken by truck to Nuevo Laredo near the US-Mexican border and coerced into the sex slave trade. The term police used was "trafficking," a topic that had been recently reported in *Newsweek* and in the major newspapers like the *Wall Street Journal* that she and Josh read religiously. The word *trafficking* was invented like those in "Jabberwocky," but its meaning implied something more terrifying.

Rosa's aunt had written that the girl's family had been able to find out where she was kept captive and they had been able to negotiate a price with an underling from the reigning cartel's family. A local "coyote" acted as the intermediary and helped in the final escape. Tia Rosita, Rosa's namesake, had been the only confidante Señora Padilla had for solace during her daughter's two-year absence.

Marcellina Padilla was reunited with her family, but in essence she came home in a cloud of shame. Her mother revealed to Tia Rosita that as her daughter's bruises healed, Marcellina confessed a deep remorse for once having had dreams of leaving her tight family circle. Even with the reality of being safe after the kidnapping, it took weeks for the girl to slowly reveal the details of the forced sex and show her mother the scars of cigarette burns on her breasts and buttocks. The mother felt her child had been ruined for life, both physically and emotionally.

Rosa thought of her own oldest daughter, Julia, dancing around the house in her pink tutu, saying, as she had since she was four years old, that she was going to be a ballerina when she grew up. But what if Julia's dreams would be cut short like Marcellina's through some terrible crime. Rosa shuddered at the thought, and determined to find out more about these kidnapped girls as she slid the letter into her writing journal.

Rosa thought of her background in an affluent Mexican family. Even if she had stayed in Mexico and married into another wealthy family, her children might never have been allowed their dreams. As it was, it had taken her long, hard arguments to persuade her very traditional father to let her go to university in the US. She was given an opportunity, but what did a poor, and now disgraced, Marcellina have to look forward to in Mexico?

The story of Marcellina continued to haunt Rosa. When John and Julia were in school and Joanie was at Mother's Day Out, Rosa went to the public library and began researching the terms "human trafficking" and "Nuevo Laredo." Her eyes were blurry from looking through the microfiche. At night she told Josh of her findings and her increasing desire to find ways to interview some of these reunited mothers and daughters.

Josh warned that it could be dangerous because he knew the cartel families guarded their sex and drug trade ferociously. He told her about a recent news article he had read detailing how Mexican federal agents captured a Guatemalan who controlled key people who used smuggling routes from Central America into the southern Chiapas state and then into the U.S. Territory through Texas. The article also mentioned the Cuestera family who controlled a widespread ground transportation operation into the US that dealt in drug and human trafficking and hired assassins including Mexican police.

Rosa listened attentively as she didn't want to put herself or her family in unnecessary danger. "Those are only newspaper reports, and you know how the press exaggerates. I don't intend to interact with any cartel family, just with the girls and their mothers," she argued with Josh. Even Josh knew when to back down from his intelligent and talented wife. Unlike Josh, Rosa seemed to act from a social consciousness honed from the contrast of her wealthy background and the impoverished *campesinos* who, she knew, were desperate for better lives. Her passion for these families was somehow wrapped up in the future of their own kids, even here in America. Josh could not really empathize with her depth of altruism. It was a far cry from his self-determined decision-making, but he did have to admire her persistence.

After the kids were settled into the new school year. Rosa told them that she needed to visit her parents in Mexico. They wanted to go too, especially John. Josh said he would hold down the fort, but with his schedules and the kids, he said jokingly, "It will be like holding the Alamo, but I can manage for a week."

Rosa arrived in Mexico that night with an affectionate welcome and a big family feast. Afterwards, she took Tia Rosita aside and explained why she had really come. She wanted to be introduced to Rosita's neighbor and her daughter. Rosa's aunt was apprehensive, but she agreed to set up a time to meet at the Padlilla home. Rosa gained their confidence by making small talk in her native Spanish. Hesitantly, Marcellina began to tell of her kidnapping from the Plaza, the drugging and transportation to a city far from her home. Rosa began to hear details of the sex trade that were even more harrowing than she had anticipated.

While the girl and women were talking, one of Marcellina's *titos* came by and asked suspiciously what Rosa was doing there. When the mother explained, the uncle said that he was the one who had brokered the girl's release through a "coyote" who transported discarded girls back home if a high enough ransom was paid to the controlling cartel. He said he could arrange for Rosa to meet Señor Pedrales for a price. Rosa wondered sadly if her home country would ever escape the mentality of bribery. But she went ahead and settled with the uncle for a $100 "consulting fee." She heard back that evening that Señor Pedrales agreed to meet her in an upscale cantiña at 1:00 the next day.

After the late dinner with the extended Munoz family, Rosa wrote postcards home in Spanish to each of the children and a special one to Josh. He had retained his fluency in the language from his post doc work in Venezuela. He never spoke much of that time except for describing his research. It seemed to Rosa to be a closed chapter of his personal life and she did not pry.

Knowing that she would get home before the postcards, Rosa decided to call home to let the children talk to their grandparents. Her mother and father were thrilled to hear John say, "*Hola, abuela y abuelo.*"

As she said goodbye on the phone, Josh cautioned her, "Rosa, don't get in over your head. These people can be ruthless and they don't care who they kill. I know this type. They only have their own purposes in mind when they act." That night Rosa thought over how she would approach the meeting with Señor Pedrales.

Señor Pedrales, the machismo coyote, needed to flaunt his wealth even though the money came from nefarious means; no sleazy roadside bar would do for him. Rosa waited in the outdoor cantiña that featured a three-foot diameter cottonwood tree surrounded by a yellow rope holding up three brightly painted wooden boxes for the squirrels. The café patrons threw their peanut shells on the floor and the squirrels scampered madly to retrieve them then ran back to their perches nibbling away at their loot while peering furtively at the people eating and drinking below. Birds flew erratically in and out of feeders while the flies buzzed persistently. After all her years in America, Rosa's sensibility of hygiene made her recoil as the black swarm converged on a piece of tortilla that lay on the floor.

Rosa's eye caught several odd-shaped fountains. One was made out of rusted pump housings, one was a simple series of buckets catching the cascading water, and a third was made out of an old wringer washing machine, reminding her of the one their housemaid had used years ago. The dripping water added a peaceful sound that would counter the serious conversation she needed to have with the transporter.

Señor Pedrales, wearing a stylish brown polo shirt as promised, found her at the designated table. They introduced themselves and Rosa tried to explain her business purpose concisely. It seemed ironic that she had to search her brain for some words in her native language. But language, as Lewis Carroll understood, is a made-up, living entity and old words can take on new meanings. When words such as "human" and "traffic" were co-joined, they took on a sinister meaning for young girls and a promise of wealth for this "coyote" sitting so calmly before her. The upshot of their brief meeting was that Señor Pedrales promised to let her know when other girls were "rescued." They settled on a price of $500 US dollars if the call led to an interview with a girl and her mother. Rosa left the cantiña aware that the contact she had just set up could prove dangerous to her and her family.

On the plane home, Rosa began to formulate the outline of a novel. She decided to tell Josh only some of the details at this point allowing her family a layer of security. She realized the very real dangers of this research. It was imperative that Josh and her children know how much she loved them and that she would never willingly leave them.

Once back home, Rosa returned to the busy routine of soccer practice for John, ballet lessons for Julia and play dates for Joanie with Sue Wilson's little boy, Tommy. The carpool arrangement with her neighbor Nina gave Rosa a chance to take her hand-written notes to the public library and concentrate on her research and writing. Her goal was to publish her novel and to finish her M.A. before the kids were out of high school. Josh, she knew, was positioning himself for a move to the dean's chair. They both worked single-mindedly toward their separate goals.

Rosa scanned the newspapers daily for information on human trafficking and began to think that her original $100 for Señor

Pedrales was wasted. But a month later, she received a phone call at 9:30 PM. Luckily Josh was still at the university and the kids were in bed. It was the coyote. He said that he had just picked up an abandoned girl in her late teens in Cuidad Juarez. If Rosa could get there tomorrow, maybe he could persuade the girl and her mother to wait one day before they headed back to their small village in the Chihuahuan interior.

Rosa had always admired Josh's insistence on the highest standards for his academic papers, and she was determined that her novel would be well researched. It had to reflect the real human drama that was only hinted at in short newspaper articles. So much was left out of them that it seemed the US government did not want to own up to how porous the Mexican border was or to disclose all that it knew about human trafficking.

Rosa debated with herself about the dangers of the research she was choosing to undertake and knew she would have to leave quickly in order not to miss the opportunity for this interview. She left a hurried note to tell Josh that she had a chance to do some "research," a code word that they had worked out earlier in case the coyote ever phoned.

The next day Josh knew that he would need to call Nina to help get the kids off to school and to watch little Joanie for a day or two. He covered for his wife's absence saying she had to leave to see a dying relative in Mexico. Josh was not really comfortable with this ruse, but he understood the necessity of it. His own research had required getting into and out of the *favelas* quickly and safely. It was always mortally dangerous to tempt a powerful cartel. Yet Josh, more than most, knew how to keep secrets.

Rosa started her 1985 station wagon, "the mobily-wagon" as Joanie had nicknamed it. She checked that the tank was full and that her tape recorder and new batteries were in her handbag as she quickly drove out of University Park onto Highway 10 to I -25 and south to El Paso.

Although she was an American citizen now, she still held dual citizenship, so she brought both passports with her just in case. At this late hour the border patrol officer looked her over carefully, noticing her beautiful Mexican features and making some sexual remarks that she ignored. He checked her valid US driving license and her passport to make sure that she was not an illegal border hopper. A bit suspicious because her Spanish was cultured and not the Tex-Mex lingo he regularly heard, he finally waved her through.

Rosa arrived in Socorro at 3:00 AM, tired but running on adrenalin. Señor Pedrales was waiting beside his dented blue Chevy pick-up with a black cover stretched across the truck bed. That hardbed must have been where the girl was hidden on the ride from the pick-up point in the desert. As he motioned for Rosa to get in the pick-up, a muscular young man sporting a striped bandana emerged from the side of the building and grunted that he would guard her car for ten US dollars. Pedrales said, "Give it to him."

Señor Pedrales drove a sinuous route, backtracking several times to be sure he wasn't being followed, and finally pulled up to a small casita. First he wanted his $500 in US cash, then he told her he would be back at 9:00 AM sharp. She hoped he would keep his word because by now she had no idea where her car had been left.

Rosa thought of stories Josh had told her about some small child secreting him in and out of *favelas*, whistling ahead to another niño so the drug runners wouldn't catch them as they moved furtively from shack to shack. "It takes a certain type of *guanos* to do this work," she decided.

It was still dark as Rosa approached the door and knocked softly. The pink window curtain was drawn back slightly and then she was admitted through a dark entrance. At the end of a short corridor, a colorful *reboso*, a long wrap women usually wore around their shoulders, hung from the ceiling to act as a room divider. A single electric light lit the white-washed walls of the room, exposing a small niche in the wall that held a blue-clad Madonna and one burning candle surrounded by some rosary beads. The mother did not give her name but nodded with a weak smile to her daughter, a small-boned girl with dark wavy hair that framed frightened brown eyes. A dark bruise marred the side of the girl's attractive face. She looked cautiously at her mother who murmured soft words of encouragement to her daughter.

The young girl visibly relaxed and moved over on the narrow bed to make room for this woman who looked like her people, but was a stranger. When Rosa took out her tape recorder, the girl froze, staring again at her mother for reassurance that is was ok to tell her story. Rosa reached out her hand and tenderly took the girl's slender fingers saying softly, *"Con permiso, ahora usted esta sequira,."* Tears glistened on her cheeks, but the girl felt safe with Rosa.

As she began the interview, Rosa recalled her newspaper research about the violent city of Nuevo Loredo just over the border from Laredo, Texas. It had 90 homicide victims last year in a city of 330,000 people, including policemen. How could a girl from Socorro protect herself against those odds?

Quietly, Rosa began to ask Carmelita questions. How did she get from her village to the Nuevo Lardeo? Carmelita described how she and some friends had been holding arms, as is the custom, taking the evening *paseo* in the town's plaza when a black van pulled alongside them. The man asked if they wanted to make some money. The girls, properly brought up even in their circumstances of poverty, shied away quickly. But before Carmelita could turn aside, another man came up from behind her and covered her face with a rag that had a strange odor. She thought she must have slumped forward, and then the man shoved her inside his van. Carmelita was stoic as she revealed, "My friends told me they stared with disbelief then ran to tell their parents. But the only vehicle in the village, Señor Martinez's, was

up on blocks awaiting a part for the motor. No one could chase the van."

Carmelita's mother and father were distraught with fear when they heard what had happened, hiding their anger and, days later, their resignation at the sad realization that their daughter had been kidnapped. Taken by whom and to where they had no idea, for few were literate in this small village, and newspapers with local and national crimes were not part of daily information. For months, then a year, and then two years, the family lived without knowing their daughter's plight.

Mama interrupted at this point and said softly, "Then a man came to our house asking if we wanted to get Carmelita back. He said it would cost 500 US dollars. Where could we get that kind of money?" The parents were bewildered at such a sum but told him to come back. Using the only working phone in the village, they placed a collect call to a cousin who had his green card and was working as a skilled marble cutter in Texas. They begged him to wire the money to Cuidad Juarez. The cousin was aware of the human trafficking problem across the Texas-US border but had not been told of Carmelita's kidnapping. Through no fault of her own, her disappearance reflected badly on the family, so little was said after the first few months. But family was family, and the cousin finally found a way to wire the money.

As Rosa heard the rest of the details from the daughter and her mother, she understood that Carmelita's transition back into the social fabric of this small town would be almost impossible. The young girl would be considered tainted goods, destined to life as a spinster, completely disregarded. The large cartels who organized the taking, using, and discarding of these village girls understood well the effects on them and their families, but money was all that was important. Many girls were disfigured or murdered, while a few lucky ones like Carmelita at least had the support and love of a tight-knit family and perhaps the few friends who had been with her that day.

The coyote came to pick up Rosa at the designated time and seemed in a hurry to get her back to her car. As Rosa drove home, she was sobered by the realization that no work of fiction could outdo the reality of this kind of tragic human drama. Yet a non-fiction work would put too many innocent people and their families in jeopardy. It was going to take some skillful writing, and she set her mind to do it.

The next night in bed, Josh listened to her story and again cautioned Rosa to be careful. One of the things Josh appreciated about Rosa, even in her role as stay-at-home mom, was the intellectual discussions they had. Josh explained, “The hubris of the top cartel honchos will know no bounds. What is a young girl to them?”

“Hubris?” Rosa queried. “Josh, do you mean like that mafia episode on TV. The one when the godfather is taking his daughter to look at a college when he spots an old rival. Remember? While the girl was at her meeting, the father killed a rival he just happened to recognize to settle an old mafia score. God, what chilled me was that he simply drove back to get his daughter and they had a lovely ride home talking about upcoming college days. That other man’s life didn’t count, only the need for the murderer’s control. How could a loving father separate the parts of his life that way? I don’t understand what kind of personal ethics could drive that kind of choice.”

Josh seemed non-committal commenting, "It is only TV fiction – their way to portray evil."

A few months later, Rosa was reading a research article called "Evil: Why people go wrong." Rosa took notes on the psychiatrist's conclusions that we all have the capacity for evil, but the potential only becomes a reality in some persons.

That night in bed, Rosa summarized the article for Josh. "Evil," she explained, "isn't the absence of empathy and compassion as evidenced by sociopaths who know full well what they do and enjoy the pain of others. Evil is when one exhibits hubris, or extreme self love." Rosa turned toward Josh, "Do you think that character trait is so strongly embedded in their psyche that no one, not even those they purport to love, would be spared if push came to shove? Do you think they ever really loved the person they killed?" Josh didn't say much as he listened in the darkened room.

Rosa went on, "Well, the author argues that killers simply dehumanize their victims at the time and discard them as cargo. Ugh, I hate that word," Rosa said. "I think 'cargo' is the only image the cartels have for their discarded Mexican girls."

Her psychologist husband finally responded, "Some people act, not from cold-hearted emotions, but from cold-headed cognition. Individuals with hubris know their victims. And you are right, they probably once loved them. I don't think they dehumanized or demonized those loved ones – their loved ones just got in the way. These people simply carry out their acts, not as evil per se, but for self-preservation."

"Hmm," Rosa murmured, "Self-preservation, is that how the cartel bosses rationalize their perverted thinking?"

"Maybe," Josh smiled to himself as he turned over, signaling the end of their midnight debate. He added one last thought, "But, the evolutionary biologists are on the right track in their research. They are now saying a positive adaptation of our large brain is to act in self-centered ways." The conversation left Rosa a bit unnerved, thinking that she knew her husband well, yet he seemed so matter of fact about this aspect of evil.

As the years went by, Rosa had several other calls from the coyote. She always made plausible excuses to her kids and her neighbor about why she would just seem to disappear for a few days. Only

Josh knew the reason, and he disclosed that to no one. Eventually, Rosa felt that she had enough facts to blend into her fiction without revealing sources or personal identities, a promise that she vowed to keep for her interviewees. If the book were to be published, she would want the human stories revealed, but at the same time she hoped the cartels would not be interested in her work of fiction.

Even though Rosa was getting more and more involved in her writing, she still occasionally checked in with her first friend at Mountain State. With Sue Wilson battling her personal demons, Rosa never considered discussing the content of her novel, so they talked of kids and general things. But Sue still had a few friends in the inner sanctum of the faculty wives' club who gossiped that Rosa seemed to disappear for a day or two and they were curious to know why. Sue had no new information for them. What Sue couldn't fathom was how or why her friend, whom she knew as such a devoted mother, could just up and leave for a few days. She could have asked Josh, but their paths never crossed anymore. That door seemed to have closed after Paul had left town. Sue couldn't be bothered to find out more as she coped daily with her failed marriage and her continuing dependency on alcohol.

Chapter 7

It Comes to Pass

In 1989 Rosa finally enrolled for her M. A. at Mountain State. As wife of a faculty member, she got a break on tuition and that helped pay for childcare. Even though Rosa was now more content, she sensed restlessness in Josh who had hoped to leave this small liberal arts college for a tier-one institution back east. He had landed a couple of interviews, but so far no firm offer had been tendered. This lack of acknowledgement of his achievements was beginning to build up to a crescendo of frustration - something Josh could not yet define.

One night in late February, Rosa was beaming as she served Josh his favorite dinner: roast beef, mashed potatoes, homemade gravy and fresh green beans. He wondered at the twinkle in her eyes while the kids all ate and talked noisily among themselves. Their family meals had always been times of sharing the day's events-teachers, sports, dance and laughter. Tonight was no exception.

After dinner, while the kids were doing their washing up chores, Josh asked Rosa, "What's up? You've been all smiles tonight." "Aren't I always?" she bantered, fluttering her dark brown eyes. She answered the quizzical look on his face with, "I'll tell you tonight in bed."

"Oh god," he thought to himself, "she's not pregnant at this late date?" Becoming department chair had only bumped his salary by $4000 a year. And if his summer travel grant to do comparative studies on the *favelas* in Brazil did not come through, he might have to postpone his research.

In his normal fashion, Josh processed everything through his own needs -- physical and mental. Spiritual was not a word that would characterize him, and he was somehow secretly proud of that fact. When he married Rosa, he had agreed that Rosa could give their future children a traditional Catholic upbringing. He covered his own lack of faith with a veneer of religious pretense that kept up appearances for Rosa's family. But personally, he knew the fruitlessness of superstitious religious beliefs that bolstered the poor peasants he had studied during his post-doc in Venezuela. He prided himself that his intellect was above all that nonsense.

That night Rosa snuggled a littler closer and whispered, “Guess what?”

“What?” he sighed with a slight tone of resignation.

“I heard from my…”

“Doctor?” Josh interrupted.

“No, silly, from my editor! My book is going to be published and they are sending me an advance of $5000. Can you believe it? Maybe you won’t have to travel to South America this summer and can spend some time with us.”

Josh pulled her closer. On one level, he was genuinely proud of her and knew he had picked a prize to pass on his genes. On the other hand, feelings of wounded pride swept over him. “I’m the one who needs to publish a new book. How dare you?” he bristled to himself. But in the darkness, his only words were, “I’m so proud of you. I love you.” She turned to him and they made quiet, intense love, a tender coupling that comes from being together for so many years. She closed her eyes and fell into a light slumber as was her pattern while Josh lay there feeling unfulfilled but beginning to think of a way out.

PART FOUR

Chapter 8

The Escape 1990

"A man consumed with hubris seldom thinks of his own suicide, instead thinks of another's homicide." Jean Forzano

June 4, 1990

The semester ended in mid-May and Josh was absorbed with getting two new papers out to the journal reviewers. He used his time efficiently because it was already early June and the kids would be out of school next week. Tonight, he told Rosa he would stay home with John and Joanie while she took Julia to her dance class. This was the night he had been planning for the last four months, ever since the news about Rosa's book.

Rosa had already left in the mini-van to take Julia and Annie Schultz, the next-door neighbor girl, to ballet class that ran from 6:30- 8:30 PM. She would go to the public library near the dance school and work on revisions of her novel that had already been accepted by the publisher.

John was doing his homework up in his room with the stereo booming as only a seventeen-year-old could tolerate. Josh knocked loudly on the door, "John, do you mind watching Joanie for a while? I forgot a reference for my paper that I have to get out of the university library." John gave an inward smile at his dad's usual way of getting out of the house when it suited him. "I'll call you from my office."

Josh arrived at his department at 6:45 PM and made sure that he said hello to Tom Dickerson. Tom made the university office his second home even when the regular term was over. He always contended that he got more work done at night, but being a bachelor he really had few reasons to go home to an empty house. Josh knew that Tom would never backtrack down the hall to check if he came back to his office that night. Besides, Josh knew you couldn't see the light from under his office door nor through the small window covered by a poster from the inside. Josh always chose to work by the small brass lamp on his desk, creating a den-like atmosphere. Josh called John to tell him that he was going to the library and asked him to put Joanie to bed at 8:00.

Then Josh leaned over to the bookshelf near his desk reaching behind the double-stack of books and pulling out his well-worn leather journal tucked behind the large tome *History of Psychology*. That night he wrote intensely about Rosa, their relationship in the past, the present news of her book's acceptance, and then he outlined what the future needed to be. He replaced the journal behind the second row of books.

Josh quietly closed his office door and headed for the library which had just started the first summer session hours. He used the students' pay phone in the hallway to call Nina Schultz to ask if she could pick up the girls saying that he was delayed at the university and didn't want the girls to have to wait at the Art Center at night. Nina said it was no problem to pick them up.

Then Josh purposely walked over to say hello to Vicki Bernstein, the librarian, who was getting books ready for the first summer session. She had always gone out of her way to help him.

"Hi, Dr. Blagsdale," she said, "What can I do for you?"

"I need to check the stacks for a reference," he said. She let him through the turnstile reserved for staff, faculty and graduate students. No one else was in the stacks at that time of night, so Vicki went off to help another patron. After a few minutes Josh let himself out the special faculty-only exit.

It was 7:30 when Josh drove calmly to the Public Library and found Rosa sitting at a table near the back. Even though she was finishing the final edits of her novel, she had enrolled in an independent seminar that had started two weeks ago, one of the first for her master's degree that she had put on hold for so long. The library was fairly deserted and he made sure no one had seen him. "Rosa," he called softly so as not to startle her. She looked up from her notepad and smiled, then said,

"Aren't you supposed to be with John and Joanie?"

“It's ok,” he countered, "I had to run to my office to get a reference and John said he didn't mind putting Joanie to bed. So how are the edits and the paper going?"

Josh looked at his beautiful wife. She had aged gracefully and seemed more poised and self-confident than ever with her dark hair slightly graying. "We haven't had much time alone, and I thought we could take a ride and get a cup of coffee. I called Nina Schultz and she said she would pick up the girls."

"Josh, I really have to get this paper finished, I want an "A" in this class. All those young kids make me nervous, with their cavalier attitude, yet they seem to come through with brilliant writing in the end."

"Rosa, you know you are smarter than all those students, plus your life experiences and work at Brandon sets you miles above them. Come on, let's go get a bite to eat. I'll make sure it doesn't have 'a chalky undertaste.'" This was a code phrase they had used since seeing *Rosemary's Baby* back in the 70's, referring to the last bite Mia Farrow took before the devil possessed her body. To Rosa and Josh, the silly phrase signaled needing some time together before they both got crazed with work and kids and needed an exorcism of their own to renew their love and friendship. Josh's charming smile accentuated his crystal blue eyes, a look that had always melted her heart. Rosa gave a chuckle and packed up her bookbag. As they started to leave, Josh noted the librarian and gently diverted Rosa down another aisle and then out the door. He was certain no one had seen him entering or them leaving.

Once in the Subaru, Josh headed toward the edge of town. " Are you really hungry?" he asked.

"Not really, we just had supper." she replied, always conscious of her petite figure.

"Well then," he coaxed, as if just thinking up this idea on the spur of the moment, "I was just thinking… I told John and Julia that I would help cut the branches of the tree out back so they can build Joanie a tree house for her birthday. I really need to get the chainsaw up at the cabin. Let's drive up there. It's only 30 minutes from town."

Rosa had started to relax, "Well, if you're sure Nina is picking up the girls. I wouldn't want them waiting outside at night alone."

"She promised it was no trouble and she will be there by 9:15 when they get out," Josh assured her.

Josh kept the car at a steady pace as they relaxed a bit and began to talk easily. It seemed that most of their daily conversation was centered on the children, and he had been extremely busy in his new position as chair of the Psychology Department. He asked Rosa to tell him the specifics about her seminar. He took her hand tenderly as he told her how proud he was of the offer she had just received for her novel. He told her not only how proud he was of her superb writing, but how brave she was to tackle the topic she had chosen, even if it had meant those tense times she had to leave unexpectedly and the danger it had put her in. "I'm glad that's over," Josh said as he squeezed her hand affectionately.

"So am I," Rosa sighed, "I hated leaving you and the kids even for a few days at a time."

Rosa was quiet for a while, enjoying the drive and the brilliant night stars as they turned off the interstate, then drove past the little mountain town of Creekside, and, finally, came to the turnoff for the cabin. Her husband had always had a bit of an edgy personality, but tonight he seemed exceptionally calm. Josh had gone into a funk a few years ago when he had applied for a position at The University of California, Santa Barbara, a Research

I institute. He came in second in the interview process. When the provost heard that Josh was seriously looking to leave Mountain Sate, he offered him the dean's position with a significant raise in pay. Josh took the promotion, but with some chagrin. Now, Rosa wondered just how much her book acceptance really bothered Josh despite his enthusiastic compliments. With Josh, one never knew for sure.

Josh unlocked the door to the cabin. Rosa went to start a fire in the fireplace where they always left the logs stacked in a little pyramid ready to light. They enjoyed the little cabin rituals that took them out of their daily suburban routine. Josh got out a bottle of Merlot and they sat on the couch and cuddled. After one long and passionate kiss, Josh took Rosa's hand and led her toward the bedroom. Without the kids around, they had time for the slow foreplay of their early years and heard each others' sweet sounds of love. After the flush of climax, Josh whispered to Rosa to doze a bit as she liked to do. She nuzzled against him and turned on her side, soon breathing evenly. Josh quietly got out of bed and grabbed his clothes. He changed in front of the fire and then went quickly to the side door. The night stars were brilliant despite the full light of the moon that shone his way to the shed. He rummaged around in the shed, but did not pick up the chainsaw. Instead, he picked out a thick two-foot piece of wood that he had measured to fit the width of the fireplace. He also took the roll of plastic wrap he had bought last summer to put on the small garden to stop the weeds, but he had never gotten around to that chore.

Entering the cabin quietly, Josh turned the doorknob to the bedroom. Looking at his wife one last time, he realized that he must dispatch her with only one quick blow to the head. He aimed from above his shoulder and let the wooden club hit the side of her head. Before any bleeding could mar the sheets, he picked up her limp body, spread out the plastic sheeting and rolled her into it. He realized what a tiny, delicate woman he had loved all these years as he lifted her lightweight body. So as not to leave any blood stains, he carefully folded the ends of the plastic as he laid her carefully in the trunk of the car.

Josh got in the car and headed back to the highway when he noticed the gas tank was almost on empty. He cursed himself for not paying more attention to details. After all, he had begun planning this night not long after Rosa had told him about her book offer. That affront became the impetus for his plan. As Josh came to the crossroad of the main highway, however, he was in luck. The gas station was still open.

Josh pulled up to the pump and filled up, but he knew that he couldn't use his credit card, which could be traced, so he had to walk inside to pay in cash. Josh hid his dismay as he saw through the window Ted Thompson, a kid he knew from Creekside, working the late shift.

It was almost closing time and Ted was just balancing the register for the night when Josh walked into the old gas station. Ted greeted him with the air of a young man who owns his small world. "Hi, Dr. Blagsdale," Ted said as he took the cash. "Are you just coming back from Creekside?

"I just needed to check something at the cabin," Josh mumbled.

"That's okay. It gets kind of lonely on this late night shift," Ted replied, excited to talk to the professor about his plans for next year. "Say, did you know that I'm graduating tomorrow night and then I'll be heading to college in town? I've already got my acceptance to Mountain State. Hope I get you for one of my classes. I want to study engineering but thought I'd try a bit of psychology on the side."

"That's a bit of an odd choice," Josh replied.

Ted shook his head shyly and said, "Yeah, but you kind of inspired me when I came up to visit with John last summer and we talked."

"I had forgotten that," Josh answered, anxious to be on his way.

"By the way," Ted added, "Tell the kids to come ride horses when you get up to the cabin this summer."

"I'll tell them," Josh said as he retrieved his receipt. "Thanks for the compliment, and good luck."

As Josh prepared to drive away, he mumbled to himself, "Nosy kid," and drove down the dark highway. Then he suddenly pulled the car onto the gravel shoulder of the highway. He realized that the Thompson kid would be the only witness to his whereabouts if, by some odd chance, they would ever find Rosa's body. He made a quick check for a highway patrol, then made a u-turn and circled back to the gas station. Josh turned off his headlights as he slowly drove into the clump of trees behind the station where the boy kept his pick-up truck and waited.

At 10:30 PM sharp Ted headed out the back door, forgetting to turn off the main pump lights, too excited with his thoughts about seeing Mary and the graduation party tomorrow. He was just about to open the door of his truck when Josh hit him with the same heavy log he had used to kill Rosa. With the left-over plastic, Josh wrapped Ted's body tightly and nudged him into the trunk on top of Rosa's corpse.

Josh returned to the interstate but turned off at marker 61 and headed east toward the rustic campsite he and Paul had found one day when trying out some new back roads. Nothing was out there but rattlesnakes, not even any potsherds for amateur anthropologists. Up on the mesa they had found an interesting bore hole and not much else. They removed the rotting board over the hole and then replaced it so that some small animal might not fall in. The two friends enjoyed the remoteness of the Rio Seco Arroyo campsite that made it feel like their own hideaway. They had never told their wives exactly where it was located.

Josh left the car at the turnoff, not wanting any fresh tracks near the campground. First he pulled the boy out, and then he lifted out Rosa's body. He put the boy's body back in the car and began the trek down the arroyo. As he walked down the dry creekbed, careful not to fall over boulders and branches, he thought about his Rosa. "My sweet Rosa," Josh mumbled to the darkness of the sidewalls, "so intelligent and brave that it frightened me deep inside. I loved that potential in you from the beginning, but you have blossomed and grown. And I, I have just stagnated. All my plans were put on hold. I know yours were too, but you waited it out with our kids, then you pounced. I admire that. But, I can't seem to get to the next level, not with you competing with me. I know you didn't mean to, but it has happened, hasn't it? There was just no other way."

Josh side-stepped a small stagnant pool of water being careful of the slippery rocks. His mind had already begun to reminisce and he knew that he would deeply miss Rosa's cheerful companionship, their late-night discussions, and her loving maternal instincts. Yet, Josh knew some things just needed to be taken care of.

After another ten minutes, Josh found the horizontal shelf he had spotted last year, a sedimentary layer carved out by some ancient flash flood. With care, he took Rosa's slight form and unwrapped her slight body one last time and he slipped off only her inscribed wedding ring. He placed her bulky cell phone in a crevice berneath the shelf and carefully rewrapped her form using the duct tape he had brought from the car. He wedged the body tightly into the shelf, pushing it in farther with the bloody log. In the last opened spaces, he sandwiched several large, flat stones he had found earlier while scouting out this burial ground and had stockpiled here last month. No tears marked his stony face, but adrenalin rushed through his body as he made the trek back down the arroyo.

Josh pondered where to put Ted's body. Then he remembered the mine shaft on top of the mesa. Back at the car, he made a makeshift travois for the athletically-built boy to pull his body to the top of the flat hill. He moved away the old rotting boards and managed to upend the body over the opening. With a final shove, Josh heard his cargo fall to the bottom of the shaft. He re-covered the hole and used some nearby piñon branches to disguise any disturbance. On the walk back to his car, a light drizzle began to fall. He looked at the heavens and hummed softly an ancient

Venezuelan rain chant, knowing that his footprints would soon be obliterated. By the time he was back on the highway, the rain began a steady downpour. It was time to get home to his kids.

Josh let himself in the house quietly since it was after midnight and John was asleep on the couch. He roused his sleepy teenager who asked, “Where is Mom?”

“I don’t know,” Josh replied. “She must have stayed late at the library. Did Julia get home ok?”

“Yeah,” said John, getting up and wrapping the quilt around himself.

“Go to bed now. I’ll go check on your sisters.”

Josh looked into Julia’s room to find his sleeping teenage daughter. Julia had her mother’s long, dark, wavy hair and big brown eyes, yet she had inherited his lithe body form, so essential for the dancer she hoped to be. He never gave much thought until now that Julia, who was particularly close to her mother, might have been upset when Nina Schultz picked them up instead of her mom.

But Josh knew the girls hadn't had to wait long in the partially lit parking lot outside the dance studio.

Josh was unaware of the testy conversation Julia had had with her brother when she got home. She asked her brother if he knew where their mom was and John had answered brusquely, "No, why should I be the one to keep track of the grown-ups? Isn't it supposed to be the other way around? Mom went to the library. Dad left for the college about 6:30 to go get a book or something and left me babysitting Joanie once again." Julia ignored John's moodiness that seemed to grow more sullen every day and headed upstairs to bed.

As Josh settled into bed, he knew that tomorrow would be the hardest day of the new life his actions had precipitated.

Chapter 9

The Graduation

11:50 P.M. June 4, 1990
Sheriff Mannie Gonzales put in a call to Bill Murphy to say that when George Valdez was coming home from his night shift at the hospital in town, he had reported that the lights at the Gas Station were still on.

Gonzales had driven out the fifteen miles from Creekside to the interstate to check it out. Ted Thompson's truck was still behind the building and the garage was locked up, but the boy was nowhere to be found. The Sheriff called Joe Thompson to see if he thought Ted might have driven to town with some high school buddies. After all, tomorrow – no today now – was graduation and the seniors might be out on their last fling.

Joe curtly answered the sheriff, "It's not like Ted to forget any details about his work. He's a responsible eighteen-year-old and has worked for Murphy's for two years now. Sheriff, I'll call you just as soon as he gets in and tell him about forgetting to shut off the main lights."

"The thing is, Joe, I've checked around and everything has been quiet tonight." Sheriff Gonzales hung up hoping the mystery would solve itself.

Joe put down the phone, with only a small niggle of worry. Then he went upstairs to make a quick check in his son's room. The bed was undisturbed and no clothes were on the floor. Ted hadn't been home after work or before going out. He remembered when he was eighteen and had done some impulsive things – just like his son sometimes did. Maybe Ted stayed with a friend and would just go directly to graduation practice at the football field. "Well," thought Joe, "graduation practice started at 8:30 A.M. and none of the seniors would miss that even if they come with a hangover."

June 5th Graduation Day

Graduation day had come and gone. Ted Thompson had not been found the previous night or all of today. It was 11:00 PM as Nora Thompson lay down on her bed, her whole being exhausted with worry. Sleep had always been her escape from the too quiet life in this small mountain town. With the Valium the doctor had given her for shock that afternoon, she thought relief would come quickly.

Nora closed her eyes for a brief second and felt her body begin to relax. She remembered the day a few years ago when Ted was a freshman. She was coming home from work in town and saw the school bus stop up ahead. A lone boy got out with a pack on his back and his jacket slung over his shoulder. He wore his old scruffy boots but didn't have on the cowboy hat most of the boys his age wore like a uniform. She stopped to pick up the mail and then caught up with him about a half mile from the ranch. "Hi Ted, do you want a ride?'"

"No thanks, Mom," he said as he tossed his pack and coat into her car. "This is my special time to enjoy the prairie and look at the mountains. I get my best thinking done on this walk." Nora drove on home, giving her adolescent son growing room.

Nora forced her mind to the present and reviewed the visit earlier that evening from her neighbors, Shirley and Hank Konic. They had come by to express their condolences – no, she recoiled, that was a word for the dead and she would not let that thought enter her mind. They only expressed their concern and hoped that Ted would be telephoning them soon. They tried to lighten her growing apprehension by describing the graduation they had just attended.

The small, rural high school gym was bedecked with streamers in the school's athletic colors of maroon and white with symbols of Harry the Gila Monster, the school mascot. Mr. Fazzuli, the principal, didn't know whether to call attention to Ted's absence or not; he was hopeful the sheriff would find the boy the next day. So instead, he called for everyone's attention – all grandparents, godparents, aunts and uncles who came from near and far to crowd into the bleachers, while the parents and siblings had the privilege of reserved seating on the gym floor.

The jazz band played some rousing songs, and unless you knew, you would not have missed one drummer in the back row. The lights dimmed while the class officers showed a slide show on a creaky old machine that sometimes balked. It featured the senior class, most of whom had been together since grade school. The room was filled with warm, funny poses, nostalgic, even sad. Living in a rural community, it was not unusual to lose classmates to a farm mishap or a highway accident. Two had died that way and they were remembered through their photos. The pictures of Ted came on the screen showing him in his football uniform and another in his jeans, bare-headed as usual, leaning against the homecoming float. The audience fell eerily silent. In a town this small, word gets out in a hurry, and Mary Hannigan, Ted's graduation partner who was forced to walk alone to her seat, had done her part to spread the news of his mysterious absence.

Next came the time for speeches, and the valedictorian, Susan Jalinky, gave a heartfelt advisory to make the most of life. She encouraged her friends to try their best whether they were going on to college or not – because, she concluded, "Life could be cut short, and our accomplishments need to start tomorrow."

Mr. Fazzuli glanced nervously at the other dignitaries on the stage and walked to the podium. He said quickly that there would not be a salutatorian speech this evening and gave no other explanation. The band began to play the graduation song softly so as not to overshadow the calling of names. The class of 1990 filed forward to receive their diplomas; Ted's name was omitted from the list.

The seniors had their graduation gowns buttoned only at the neck allowing the rest of the robe to flutter open as each student proudly walked up to receive a diploma and shake the required hands. The audience could see snippets of various dress and shoes – their final statements of personal style. There were short-shorts and old tennis shoes, a tailored cowboy shirt and wide belt buckle with boots polished for the occasion, even one sleek black dress complemented by obviously uncomfortable high heels. Then the graduates changed over their tassels, and hats were thrown up in unison.

After the gym floor cleared, a small group of Ted's close friends exchanged the latest rumors about his disappearance. But for most of them this was a day of optimism and the prevailing mood was "Let the partying begin." Surely, he would turn up soon.

The Konics did not stay for graduation refreshments since they really weren't close to anyone besides Ted in this year's class, but as good community members they always showed up to demonstrate their support of the local schools. They decided to stop by the Thompson's, bringing them a copy of the program and checking to see if they had any more news of Ted.

Still holding the graduation program, Nora finally fell into a drugged stupor of sorts. Later in the night, a sheer panic, like a steely sharp butcher's blade, struck through her chest. If it were another time and place, she would think she was having a heart attack. Clutching her chest, she opened her eyes to the blackness of the shuttered bedroom. She could only hear the flap of the window shade and feel the cool mountain air. Phosphorescent dials on the clock said 3:00 a.m. Tears welled in her eyes and she shuddered with uncontrollable sobbing. She had a premonition that she would never see her son again.

Chapter 10

The Fantasy of Truth

"Truth is stranger than fiction, fiction has to make sense."
Leo Rosten

Josh knew it would be tricky talking to the kids about their mom's absence, but then he had had some practice when she was off doing her research. John was the problem, always a skeptic, more like him than Josh wanted to admit. John was going to graduate from Highlands high school next week and head off for the Navy, so, reasoned Josh, if he could just get the girls to understand that their mom had chosen to leave, he would be ok.

Since it was a school day, the kids were up with their own alarm clocks as usual. Joanie and Julia got their cereal and brought it to the table in automatic fashion. John came in more awake than usual and quizzed his father, "Where is Mom? I checked the shower and your bedroom? Didn't she come home last night?

The girls tuned into the conversation intently while they listened for their dad's reply, "I don't know," he said. " I fell asleep and thought she would come home later."

"Dad, it was after midnight when you got here. Weren't you worried by then? What about now, for Christ's sake?"

"John," Josh started, but Joanie started to cry. "Where is my mom?"

"Hold on kids. Let's think about this logically. Julia, didn't your mom pick you up at 9:00 from dancing?"

"No, Mrs. Schultz did. She said you had called and said that you and Mom would both be late and you didn't want us waiting outside."

"That's right, I remember now. I was at my office getting a research paper and decided to stay a bit longer I talked to Tom Dickerson and Mrs. Bernstien. Your mom called about 7:30 on her cell phone and asked me to call Mrs. Schultz to have her pick up you and Annie."

“Well, why isn’t she home now?” Joanie whined.

“Don’t worry now,” he said as he patted Joanie’s head and turned away to make some toast to eat with his coffee.

All three children had that panicked look they had had five years ago when Rosa had suddenly begun to disappear for a few days at a time. The first time, Rosa had called from a pay phone in Brownsville, Texas, two days after she had left. She wanted to reassure the kids that she was just fine and only visiting a sick friend. They were uneasy but accepted their mom’s calm assurances.

Josh recalled another more dire time when Rosa had received an urgent phone call from Tlxacala, Mexico, from a mother whose daughter had disappeared after going into town to her job. The mother had been given Rosa Blagsdale’s name by an anonymous coyote who said someone might know where the kidnapped daughter had been taken and Rosa might be interested. The mother wouldn’t give her own name for fear of the Meninquez cartel. That time Rosa had left the house in a hurry and had made her way to the Las Cruces airport. She never knew when a lead for her research would surface and she in no way wanted her family involved in the dangerous dealings of the cartel. Her fact-based novel was being built on case studies and interviews of some of these rescued girls and their mothers, tracing their ordeals from Tlxacala to Brownsville. Some of the stories ended in brutal beatings, prostitution, and often death. A mere few had reunions with their mothers. So far her involvement had been hidden from the cartel bosses, at least she had hoped so. But money talks, and she feared someone would betray her if the price was high enough.

Josh had tried to steer Rosa away from such a controversial topic, cautioning, "Just write it as fiction, or make up the locations, don't let the family know your name." But she had become too close to a few of those mothers and their stories of anguish to heed her husband's advice. By then she had already sent a manuscript to one publishing house and the editor assigned to her had said that the intensity of the stories would make her novel so popular and marketable that it would eventually be translated into Spanish.

John interrupted Josh's memory as he sipped his coffee. "So, did Mom have to go to Mexico again?" John asked persistently. His mom had "disappeared" several times for a few days in the last five years and John knew that his father never called the police. John had asked his mom to let him read her novel. She hesitated at first but knew it would be in the bookstores soon. Even as a preteen John had been an avid viewer of world news and he understood implicitly the dangers of revealing any cartel-controlled activity in Mexico. John had inherited his mom's fluency for languages and corresponded in Spanish with one of his cousins in Guadalajara. He briefly described his mom's novel and his cousin wrote back quickly warning about the Meninquez's network that extended across Mexico to larger cities and even small villages scouring for fresh teenaged girls and young boys. José added that it was not safe to speak of such things. But now that the novel would be in print, it would be even more dangerous to his mom because the cartel has ways to find whatever or whomever they want.

"Did she leave a note this time? Let's call the police and file a missing person's report, Dad," John coaxed.

"No. Let's wait a couple days and see if she calls again like the last times. I know you're all worried, but she would just want us to carry on till she can contact us." Reluctantly, the kids got ready for school. On the way out, Josh reassured them that he would let them know as soon as their mom called.

Josh had no intention of going into the office. He had covered his bases last night by saying hello to Tom Dickerson and making sure that Vicki Bernstein had talked with him. At 7 PM Josh had disguised his voice on a pay phone to call Mrs. Ramirez's number in Tlxacala saying Rosa had new information about her daughter and that Rosa would be flying in late that night or the next day. If the police wanted to trace Rosa's cell phone calls, they would find a call to his office about 7:30. When Rosa had popped into the bathroom before they left the library and he waited in the car, he had slipped Rosa's phone out of her handbag and dialed his office number. Now the phone was hidden in a crevice in the arroyo.

Today Josh poured himself another cup of coffee and waited patiently for an inevitable call from the police. About 9:30 AM Officer Suarez called to report finding Rosa's abandoned car at the public library late last night. The car appeared undamaged but was unlocked, and a red wallet had been found with papers strewn about. Her ID was in the wallet, but no cash was found. It was probably a burglary, but the police wanted to know if his wife had reported the incident. In a worried tone, he answered, "Actually I have not seen my wife since she left the house last evening."

"Why are we just finding out about this, Dr. Blagsdale?" the officer asked suspiciously.

"It's a long story. Rosa has had to do this before for the research she is doing, but she always calls in a day or two."

"Dr. Blagsdale, I'm sending Detective Hildago to your home to get the rest of the details. In the meantime, I'm sending out an APB. And, by the way, we'll be impounding your wife's car for evidence."

"Evidence of what?" Josh whispered as an alarmed and wounded husband might.

"Murder, Doctor. In any case, we don't want to contaminate any forensic evidence."

"Ok, Officer Suarez," Josh replied, "I'll be here. I'm on summer break, so I don't have to go to the office until later."

Josh greeted the detective and his partner at the door. After answering all the routine questions, Josh established his whereabouts last night and told them where he thought Rosa was supposed to be. One officer called the public library and talked to the woman who was on duty to confirm that Rosa had been there. Josh offered the home numbers for Tom Dickerson, Vicki Bernstein and even Nina Schultz.

While they were waiting for the other officer to make the calls, Josh took the opportunity to show Detective Hildago an advance copy of Rosa's book. Hildago read the reviews on the back cover of the book jacket:

> *Stopping the modern slave traffic of humans is like trying to cut off all the arms of an octopus at once. In the last few years, 800,000 sex slaves were moved across international borders: 80% women and 20% children. Even with the banding together of law enforcement and victims' rights groups, the secrets of the international sex slave trade are closely guarded. The author's first novel is a stunning revelation of interviews with grieving mothers and their daughters, scarred victims rescued by sheer will from modern warlords. To infiltrate the cartel networks for the*

research was a dangerous task, to publish those facts shows extreme bravery."

The officer then scanned the first few pages of the book.

The girls with heavy make-up shadowing their eyes, low cut Mexican blouses and short skirts paraded in a slow circle around Calle Santo Tomas. Their artificial smiles dared not crack as the lieutenant watched vigilantly from the window in the two-story apartment across the street. Clients watched nodding and gesturing to one another. With the prospective stream of girls, it was like panning for gold. Vendors sold snacks and drinks, but no condoms. It was a fiesta of flesh.

After the men made their choices, they would be escorted into the warehouse building to curtained cubicles. By this time, his passions aroused, the client would not notice or care about the cheap beds and dirty sheets. But the child-woman knew she must first get the pesos before giving herself away again, or face the consequences.

"Pretty scary stuff your wife was into," the officer commented handing back the book. Detective Hildago was aware of the scenario because some of that human trafficking came through this state, if not yet his city. He began to wonder if they would ever find the professor's wife if she was near the border again.

"I am too aware of that," answered Josh. "She must have received a call from Mexico and left quickly for the airport. Sometimes she can warn me ahead of time, sometimes not."

The detective fished a bit, "We didn't find any passport."

Josh volunteered some information, "She usually carried both of her passports with her in a zippered pocket of her coat. If she left the car unlocked, maybe someone forced her out of it. You're the detective and I'm just guessing. But, officer, my kids will want to know something. I sent them to school hoping to have some information when they get back."

"We'll want to talk to each of them separately," the detective said as he rose to leave the kitchen.

"Why do you want to do that? They are worried enough as it is," Josh argued.

The detective looked at Josh straight on and said, "To check your alibi, Dr. Blagsdale."

Newspaper reporters had another more urgent case to sensationalize that week. The police were too busy following leads about the missing boy from Creekside, a possible murder-kidnapping; rewards were out and his classmates had mounted a manhunt. Even the FBI was involved, presuming the boy had probably been transported across state lines. The community was visibly upset so the news of a missing woman who had a habit of taking off for a couple days at a stretch was not much of a concern right then.

Even though there was nothing reported in the police blotter of the *Highlands Herald*, gossip got around the university about Rosa's car being found and the fact that she seemed to be missing. Ironically, the only mention of Rosa was in a small newspaper article about the Highlands Art Center. Rosa had volunteered as a board member over the years because of Julia's interest in dance.

In spite of missing the latest meeting as she sometimes did, the committee had re-elected Rosa to another year as treasurer.

Sue Wilson heard about her missing friend Rosa while in the hospital for another periodic dry-out. Her mother, Pat Chenango, visited with her confiding, "You know Tommy is upset, Sue."

"Because of my being in the hospital again?" she resigned herself.

"Maybe, but there is more this time," Mrs. Chenango answered. "Amy told him that Joanie's mother was missing and was probably dead. Now he thinks that when you are in the hospital, you might be dead and not come back to take care of them."

"Oh no, " Sue replied, "Is it true about Rosa, Mom?"

"I don't know. It's been a week now and the police have no leads. They asked the professor to take a lie detector test and apparently he passed it. They think she may have gone back to Mexico again."

Mrs. Chenango waited until Tommy and Amy left to get sodas in the waiting room, then she told Sue the other news making the headlines. “By the way, since you’ve have been in here, a boy, Ted somebody or other, is missing from Creekside and it was the night before his graduation. Can’t you just imagine his poor mother! Police say they’re trying everything to find him and hope someone traveling late at night on the highway hasn’t kidnapped him. The paper is just tossing up hot air theories. Nobody seems to know anything for sure. What strikes me as odd, even though we don’t know the kid, is that he disappeared the same night as Rosa.”

Sue sighed. “Mom, what connection could there possibly be? I know Rosa. She was my first friend when Paul and I came to Highlands. I just can’t imagine any reason that she would up and leave her kids. Do you think Josh could be involved somehow? But the boy from Creekside – it just doesn’t make any sense to try to link the two.”

Sue needed to get out of this hospital soon and get her act together. She wanted to be a more vigilant mother because all of a sudden life in Highlands seemed more dangerous that it had before.

The next week went by in a blur for the Blagsdale family. Detectives in and out, fingerprint samples for Josh and even John, phone records checked and a lie detector test for the husband, always the first suspect when a wife is missing. Josh prepared for it using deep meditation and bio-feedback techniques he lectured about in his psych course. He had mentally prepared and rechecked his facts as he had been so well-trained to do as an academic. As he predicted, nothing was found by the detectives.

Josh had mentioned to Detective Hidalgo that sometimes a contact from the US Justice Department's Office of International Affairs sent Rosa information. When Hidalgo called their field office in Mexico City, the OIA agent confided in the detective that Mrs. Blagsdale had been told about Lucerito Gonzales, aged 13, who had been kidnapped from her small Mexican town. Lucerito had been transported to Brownsville, beaten senseless, and left unconscious. The OIA agent said gruffly, "Yeah, all this to 'break' her so that she would be 'easier to train.'" He explained to the detective about the brainwashing of the girls so they wouldn't try to escape. The cartel had two golden rules: 1) our network will find you and cut you to pieces and 2) your family will never be safe again. The psychological hold of these threats kept the girls at their work for little or no profit. And when their bodies aged, they were finally "put out to pasture," left sick and destitute in another town without food or money. The horse-trading analogy made one sick to think of it.

Lucerito Gonzales was an exception. She sneaked away to call her mother and the OIA agent who had secured her rescue had set up an interview for Rosa with Lucerito and her mother. But the next time, the OIA agent told Detective Hidalgo, he did not call Rosa because the grapevine said the cartel was getting close to knowing her identity as an informant. Detective Hildago remarked, "Rosa had to know that she was playing with fire and would get burned alive one of these days."

The first month after her mom's disappearance was rough for little Joanie who hounded Josh daily about when her mom would be back. Julia complained about why her mom had to leave now when her first big ballet recital was coming up that weekend. Didn't her mom know how important this was to her? Josh tried to console her saying, "Adult matters sometime take precedence, and you will understand that better when you are a grown-up." That kind of explanation did nothing but make Julia more sullen.

Two months passed and Professor Josh Blagsdale occupied himself with having to go through the summer college graduation ceremony as if nothing were amiss. Little had appeared in the newspaper because the police were working on the assumption that Rosa had disappeared, as she had several times before when she was doing research for her novel in Mexico. Josh was cooperative, explaining that his wife would always call after a few days to apologize for her urgency of leaving quickly to get the interviews when she could. Josh confessed that he had known the dangers of his wife's work but that she was a determined woman and wanted to finish her work despite the threat of being identified to the cartel. In actuality, he had presumed that this alibi would play right into his personal plan.

Two months later, Josh was questioned more thoroughly by the New Mexico Bureau of Investigation and again he had covered his tracks well. Tom and the librarian corroborated his whereabouts that night. No one had seen him at the public library and the fingerprints on Rosa's car found at the library were both his and hers since they frequently exchanged cars. Rosa's cell phone was missing, so they checked the phone records to trace the call from her cell to the office. Josh's office phone records showed that he called home to John that evening. They never traced the call to their neighbor, Nina Schultz, to pick up the girls which she did.

By the end of the month Rosa's novel, *The Lost and Recovered: the Tragedy of Human Trafficking* had made the headlines. When the police read the content, they presumed it was a revenge killing by the cartel and the case of Rosa Blagsdale went into the "cold case file" until more clues might turn up. For all intents and purposes the law enforcement of the city of Highlands, the state of New Mexico Bureau, the FBI, and the OIA considered Rosa Blagsdale another victim who dared to uncover the secrets of the human trafficking slave market. No ties to any cartel family could ever be traced.

The children took longer to convince. Josh tried to cook and clean in order to establish some normalcy with the kids after his every move had been investigated time and again. He called a family meeting to tell each of the children about their mother's dangerous research for her book and the interviews she had been called out to do every time she seemed to disappear for a few days. John just scoffed saying, "Mom already told me all this and she even let me read the drafts. Do you think I'm stupid or something? Why can't they trace who kidnapped her from her own car? Are the police afraid of the cartel, too? They just wrote off my mother's death and put the records in a box to rot on some shelf." John stomped out of the kitchen, slamming the door behind him. Josh could hear the roar of his motorcycle racing out of the driveway. Josh turned toward Julia now, shrugging his shoulders at her brother's outburst.

He made another effort to explain to Julia, who was holding Joanie closely. "Your mother was very brave, you know. Think how scared those mothers in Mexico were. Yet your mom was able to gain their confidence so the daughters could tell their stories. But I think they found out who was interviewing them. The cartels have spies everywhere or they convince ordinary people to inform on them by offering them money bribes. The poverty is so bad they will do anything just to survive. It's hard for us in this country to understand that kind of desperation. Julia, I think your mother just became a victim of that vicious cycle of power and poverty."

Julia had read the latest newspaper reports about Mexican cartel and drug trafficking. "Dad, do you think they'll ever find her…?" she mouthed the word "*body*" so that Joanie wouldn't notice.

"There is always hope," Josh answered his daughter. In her mind, Julia silently forgave her mother for missing her ballet recital.

As fall approached, John, always skeptical and rebellious, was unbelieving and became more and more withdrawn. He finally showed some excitement when he told his dad that his application for the Navy had been accepted. Josh agreed that this was the best thing for his son and encouraged his choice of specialty in the intelligence sector. For John, telling his sister Julia would be the hardest part.

The next day John knocked on Julia's bedroom door. "Sis," I got accepted into the Navy and I'm leaving in two days." Julia, looked at her brother's deep blue eyes and wavy auburn hair, so much like their dad's.

"I know," she muttered. "I heard you talking to Dad."

"Will you be all right alone with him and Joanie? I'll email you as often as I can."

Julia nodded as a tear began sliding down his sister's cheek.
"You know, I don't believe the story about Mom," John said solemnly.

"Why not?" Julia asked surprised. "Don't you think all those different police departments have done everything they could?"

"What if the murderer was someone closer to home?" John replied.

Their conversation was cut short as Joanie burst into the room. "Hi guys," she said, holding her stuffed bear close to her heart. "What are you talking about?" They just laughed to deflect their somber mood. Two days later, John had packed his duffle bag and was ready to get out of Highlands and start his own life at boot camp.

PART FIVE

Chapter 11

Cheryl 1991-1997

With John off at boot camp, Josh and the girls settled into a routine. The mention of Rosa became less frequent and Josh felt that the children had come to terms with their mother's death even though there was no body to view when they held the small family memorial service. Periodically, Josh would get a call from the local police who had investigated Rosa's abandoned car about a clue that usually led to some local juvenile gang activity. There had been some jurisdictional squabbling between the city police and the county sheriff's department, but no detectives bothered to call after the initial flurry of activity. Whenever another missing person was found along the interstate, the New Mexico Bureau of Investigation would get excited, but only rarely did Josh ever hear from the FBI or OIA and only if they thought there was a lead to human trafficking and the drug cartels across international borders. In all of that combined investigative effort, Josh was no longer a prime suspect and, as John had predicted, Rosa was just one more unsolved cold case shelved away in some boxes.

Julia was older now and capable of preparing their dinner that Josh had defrosted from their freezer. She watched her little sister without much complaining until he got home. But Joanie was only nine, and she still needed more mothering than her teenage sister or a busy father could provide for a third grader. She worried about who could go on her field trips and help as a room-mother. Sometimes Joanie still cried at night and she still kept the picture of her mother by her bedside. Josh did what he could to comfort her, even giving her false hope that perhaps her mother was just hiding out in Mexico and could come back when it was safe. "When" was never defined. These circumstances convinced Josh he was cleared to move on.

Julia had resumed her ballet lessons, but when Mrs. Shultz would pick her up at night, she could never force herself to look at the spot where her mother had always parked her car while waiting. The hole in her heart was like that empty parking place, and the only way she knew to fill it was to pursue her dream of escaping to New York. Young as she was, she already had an offer to go there this summer for a student ballet internship. For now, she focused all her energy on that.

The first holidays were brittle. Fourth of July, Labor Day and then the Thanksgiving that came and went with a sad little dinner by themselves. A phone call from John cheered them up even when they heard that his first leave wouldn't be until after the new year. The fall semester ended in early December, but Josh begged off skiing with friends even though the snow up at the Red River ski area was great. Julia was self-absorbed with her newest boyfriend so her sadness seemed to slip away each day. Joanie was coming around too, trying to be cheerful, getting out all the family Christmas ornaments. But the hand-made angels and little drummer boys brought back too many poignant memories. Josh knew that what she really needed as a present was a new mother, and finding her one would seem normal for a lonely widower, a role only he knew that he had played before.

At Julia's Christmas recital Josh and Joanie sat next to an attractive woman. During intermission Josh turned toward the blonde, 30-ish woman and started up a conversation. Her name was Cheryl Rheingold and she was a nurse who had come to watch her niece's recital. Josh told her a bit about himself and the girls and mentioned that he was single. At the end of the evening, he asked if he might get her phone number.

They had a few dates of dinner and movies and Cheryl turned out to be pleasant enough company. Josh knew she had been divorced and that she regretted having missed the experience of children of her own. Josh calculated that it would be reasonable to ask Cheryl to his department Christmas party. The faculty had accepted the fact that Rosa had disappeared last May and was presumed murdered in Mexico; out of consideration for him as dean, no one brought up the subject. The party at the provost's home went well. Being a nurse, Cheryl was comfortable interacting with all sorts of people, even academics with their pointed repartee.

Josh decided that it was time to bring Cheryl into his more intimate circle of family and friends. He asked if she would like to help him and the girls cook Christmas dinner for a party of eight – the two of them, the kids, the Schultzes from next door and their two children. They would have some of their mother's traditional Mexican foods, including *empanadas* that the girls and even John had learned to cook with her.

Nina Schultz had been fairly reserved toward Josh since Rosa's death. Back in May she had resented the police intrusions at any time of day and the repeated questioning to confirm Josh's work habits. Maybe this dinner would calm down everyone's nerves.

Cheryl outdid herself, bringing her special artichoke-spinach hors d'oeuvres. The two women talked easily in the kitchen while Brad Schultz and Josh watched football and the kids kept busy playing Yahtzee. Dinner was as joyful as could be expected, with no one pointing out the obvious absence of Rosa.

The winter months passed quickly and the two families, plus Cheryl, finally went skiing a few times at Red Mountain. By that next spring, the police had still found no other evidence of Rosa, and no new leads had surfaced. All presumed her dead. Josh considered that after awhile he could cover his bases and file for a legal divorce as many MIA widows do. But for now, he simply asked Cheryl if she would like to move in with him and the girls.

Julia's emails to her brother let him know how appreciative she was of Cheryl's help at home with Joanie. She added that Cheryl had gone with her to pick out a sleek, blue dress for prom, the one in the picture with the new hairdo that she sent in the mail. Josh's older daughter was mature enough to realize how much her little sister still needed mothering, especially now that Julia would be leaving for college next fall. Nice as her dad was, Julia realized he was little help when it came to getting a bra and dealing with the obvious changes Joanie would have soon. Besides, it helped that her mom's old friends, Nina Schultz and Sue Wilson, liked Cheryl too.

John managed some leave in January and was finally able to meet Cheryl in person. Josh was secretly relieved by his son's more mature attitude. It seemed that some of his bitterness and suspicion about his mother's death had worn off or was well-hidden by his new military bearing. John was now involved in courses for Naval Intelligence and he shared his dreams with Julia who was getting ready to graduate and finally head to college and dancing in New York.

Cheryl proved to be a good mate during the next six years even though they never married, and Joanie blossomed under her care into a well-rounded teenager. Julia wrote frequently to her little sister and sent pictures of her ballet training and performances in

New York. She never mentioned to her dad the emails she and John exchanged that stated emphatically she would never go back to New Mexico because of the memories of her mother's murder.

As calm as he appeared on the surface, Josh was becoming restive again. Maybe it was just the bleakness of another winter. Joanie would graduate next spring and he would still be here – dean at a middling university. He wanted more. By now he knew that Cheryl was smart in a practical way, but intellectually she would never fit in with faculty wives at a larger university. Even though she was educated, she was not really quick-witted, and anyone could pick that up in her conversations that often turned to the mundane. He knew he would eventually need someone more his intellectual equal, and he began to devise a solution.

In the next few weeks, Josh's conversations with Cheryl bordered on the sarcastic. He found fault with small details and Cheryl rebuked him saying, "Why are these petty things bothering you now? Am I doing something different?"

Josh subtly suggested that maybe she wasn't as efficient at work as she used to be. When they went out together, he never complimented her dress and seemed to ignore her attempts at conversation. Her confidence began to lag, and she confided her despondency to one of her nurse friends.

At 6:30 AM Wednesday morning February 3rd, Josh quietly approached Cheryl as she slept soundly in their bed. She had worked the night shift and often took a Benedryl to get a good six hours sleep. Earlier, in the garage, he had found a slim piece of pipe with a protruding point and wrapped it in cloth. Cheryl's head was turned to the left when he swung the pipe with one definitive blow. Wiping up the small ooze of blood with the cloth, he carried her out to the car and carefully positioned her head with the pinpoint bruise facing down to look like it had hit the steering wheel. Using disposable lab gloves, Josh taped a hose to the exhaust pipe and into the window, then started the motor. There would be no note to incriminate him.

As he pulled his own car out of the garage, its noise muffled the sound of the motor from Cheryl's car. He pushed the switch to close the garage. On the way across town he pulled off the interstate and tossed the pipe, rag and gloves into the fast flowing river. The evidence swirled away toward the downstream sewer.

Joanie had spent the night with friends, and his secretary had him scheduled for a meeting across town to discuss the expanding role of the university in the community. He arrived 15 minutes early, set up his PowerPoint, now all the rage for presentations, had coffee and chatted with old friends. Promptly at 9:00 AM the meticulously dressed professor called the group to order in his confident tone, "Ladies and gentlemen, shall we begin?"

Josh was back at his office by 10:30 AM, busy with his normal workload, keeping his usual custom of not taking a lunch break. At 2:00 PM Josh's secretary knocked at his office door. "Dr. Blagsdale, I just got a call from your neighbor, Mrs. Schultz. She said that you have to get home right away. The police are at your house."

Josh let a worried look cross his face and said quickly, "Is Joanie ok?"

"I think it's Cheryl, Dr. Blagsdale, but Mrs. Schultz just said to hurry," the secretary replied, wondering about her distraught boss.

Josh calmly drove to his house knowing precisely what he would see. His demeanor changed appropriately as he pulled up in front, out of the way of the ambulance. "What's going on?" he asked the EMT as the young man put the gurney into the back of the ambulance.

"Not sure. We found her slumped over the steering wheel and a hose connected from the exhaust pipe and taped into the front window. The engine was running. Looks like she tried to commit suicide."

The police photographer was taking a close-up picture of Cheryl's head, zooming in on the bruise on the left side where she apparently had hit it when falling forward. Detective Wingate took Josh aside and said, "You need to come down to headquarters with us."

"Did she leave a note?" Josh asked.

"We'll talk at headquarters," he said. "Follow us in your car."

Knowing he would have to take a lie detector test again, Josh breathed deeply and rehearsed his story on the way to the station. He would say that he had received a call from Cheryl's supervisor who thought she seemed to be under a lot of pressure and should take some time off. This would be easy to confirm. More hidden had been Josh's subtle undercutting of Cheryl's self-confidence that took several months to effect, but in the end, his ploy had worked. He lied to her when he said that a firm job offer had come through and he would be leaving next year. She said that she would quit her job and come with him, but he countered that she was too old for them to consider getting married and starting over with a young family. Cheryl seemed devastated, and her reaction played right into his plan.

Josh had to be especially attentive to Joanie in the following months as she dealt with yet another death at her tender years. But of his three of the children, the youngest had his purposeful set of mind and survival instincts, although in her, it was blended with Rosa's intelligence, temperament and compassion. Joanie would cope again as he became the concerned father. John and Julia were too far away for his immediate concern.

Chapter 12

Folie de Grandeur March, 1998

Normally, the system of arroyos leading to Rio Seco Arroyo looked like fractured puzzle pieces, dry and cracked, while the basalt-capped mesas of volcanic origin hovered silently in the background. The solitude, occasionally punctuated by the song of a meadowlark, was broken by an eerie sound coming from half a mile upstream. A sudden crest of spring floodwaters moved like a cranked-up conveyor belt. The water, stained blood-red from hematite, quickly eroded away any rocks it encountered, scouring out the side ledges and turning the once dry arroyo into a screaming rage, excavating over twenty thousand cubic feet of earth in less that an hour. Water erupted from the side creeks, and the main course began to look like a battleground exposing naked bedrock and sun-bleached branches stacked waist deep. The entire geometry of the creek became a tangle of boulders. Miniature waterfalls formed, ravishing lush nests of spring grass growing in quiet pools. As devastating as this spring storm might be, its violence would uncover hidden secrets.

A few days later the Southwest landscape would be nourished by deposits of fresh nutrients but then become desiccated once again. The searing sun with a 99-degree temperature didn't stop two boys out on their bikes searching the arroyo for treasures that might have washed up after the flood. They found a mirror torn off an old car abandoned somewhere up stream. The horns of a deer were wrapped around a cottonwood trunk, but they couldn't dislodge them. They climbed down into the creekbed to retrieve a man's old leather wallet protruding out of a mound under the ledge of rock. It was still moist and smelled of mildew as they opened it to reveal no identification and, worse, no money. Since they were already off their bikes, they decided to explore the area a bit more. Fred yelled at his buddy Pedro to come take a look at this thing wrapped in plastic. Pedro stooped down to peel back the shredded strip when he shrieked with fear.

"Oh my god, *Dios mio* , it is a body! Eewh, there is a ring on the bony finger."

Pedro and Fred scrambled up the arroyo bank and sped home on the bikes to their home. The boys excitedly spilled out the story of the dead person. Pedro's mother said they must report this to the *policia* immediately so the boys would not be in trouble.

"But, Mama," Pedro pleaded, "Tio Jose is still illegal. We don't want no police nosing around."

"Could you tell if is was a man or a woman, hijo?"

"No," replied the boy still shaken by the corpse.

"We have to do what is right. Call them," Mrs. Garcia said in a resigned voice.

The next day the local headline read, "Woman's Body Washed out of Rio Seco Arroyo." The news article told about the two boys finding the body and reporting it to the police. It said that dental records would be compared to help identify the body. Josh folded the morning newspaper so that the headline wasn't glaring when Joanie came in for breakfast.

A week later the New Mexico Bureau of Investigation confirmed it: the body was that of Rosa Blagsdale. Detective Hidalgo had not yet retired and was called in on the case once again. He wondered if the Mexican cartel had tracked her down in her own backyard and killed her right under their noses. As a cop, he knew that without solid evidence, he could not rule out that or other possibilities. But for the time being, the husband was once again the prime suspect.

Josh was detained, but his lawyer got him out for lack of evidence. Detective Hidalgo warned him to stay within reach and not to leave the vicinity.

Josh seemed morose and spent more and more time at the university. Joanie didn't know how to communicate with her father. She wrote to Julia to commiserate but got a rather indifferent response. Julia's reply indicated that she had other things to worry about now. Joanie even called John once, but he was away on assignment. She didn't know if he knew about their mom's body being identified or about the police exhuming Cheryl's body. When the Navy eventually contacted John, he had not been totally surprised. Joanie chalked up his coldness to his military training in intelligence. It seemed to her that nothing much shocked her brother, especially now that he had returned from Afghanistan. But this was their step-mother, even if John had not known her very well. She worried that the insensitivity of war may have made her brother much more like their father.

As a high school senior who wanted to be a political scientist, Joanie read the newspapers diligently. More and more details were appearing about the deaths of her mother and Cheryl. She was beginning to doubt the facts as she had known them all this time, but she couldn't bring herself to confront her father who had only shown her deep love and compassion, especially as the two of them were alone this last year after Cheryl's presumed suicide.

One night Joanie decided she needed a break from the publicity pressures and called a friend to go out to a movie. It started at 7:00 PM and she would have a few hours without scrutiny and whispered remarks purposely loud enough for her to hear. She could sit in the darkened theater and not have to answer questions from curious people, friends and neighbors included. She said to herself. "My too-bad-dad," as she had taken to calling him in her dark moments, "will just have to fend for himself tonight."

Since being dismissed by the police at this time, Josh's life at work had been a quiet hell. Everywhere he went people looked at him in disbelief. The police were sifting through every bit of evidence from Rosa's case from the time she went missing, the abandoned car, the implications of the novel, even his first lie detector test, which now, they say, he did not pass convincingly enough. As bits of news filtered to the newspaper, he felt condemned before he was even accused. And then the Cheryl business! They were going to exhume her body this week and recheck the bruise on her head. No one had even questioned her motives for suicide before, let alone considered it a murder at that time.

But deep inside himself, Josh just secretly smiled. He knew the patterns in his life that he had so carefully nurtured had come full circle. He had even planned for this eventuality. He understood his own character better than most. If anything, he resembled the drug lords who controlled the *favelas* and the cartel bosses who tossed out their used cargo with cold-hearted manipulation. He knew that a man or woman could appear as a highly functional, productive member of a society at home and in the workplace and yet lead a double life, compartmentalizing his or her needs from other's, even from loved ones. "Call it hubris, if you will," he rationalized to himself. "I call it survival."

What was so ironic about the timing of the spring flood was that he had just received a firm offer from Purdue University for the next year. Finally, his academic prowess would have been rewarded.

But it was too late now. Sooner or later the police would unravel all his alibis and it was time for his *piece de resistance*. Josh gave only passing thoughts to his son and daughters now. Days before, he had convinced himself that they would be better off never knowing.

Josh went to the locked cabinet in his closet and took out his hunting rifle, walked outside to the backyard and put the gun in his mouth.

PART SIX

Chapter 13

John

John was deployed for a second tour when he received an urgent message at his Special Forces Intelligence desk. When he asked permission from his superior, he was granted immediate family emergency leave to join his sisters at home. When details of the brutal story unfolded in the news, even those who had thought they were friends of Professor Josh Blagsdale could not condone his premeditated actions. The funeral was a simple burial. Few people attended, mostly friends of Joanie and Julia, and Josh's long-time secretary from the university.

Julia returned quickly to New York. Joanie's life was locked in a confused tussle of emotions – the love she thought she knew from her father, the love she had been robbed of from her mother, the supportive companionship she had shared with Cheryl, and now subtle accusations she felt from her siblings who thought she had stayed too loyal to her father. Joanie decided that she couldn't remain in the family home by herself, so she took Julia up on the offer to live with her in New York for the summer. It was left to John to clean out his father's office at the university.

John entered the office he had been in so many times. He switched on the brass lamp over the desk and closed the door with the poster blackening the window. He had always wondered why his dad had to create this secret sanctuary. He turned on the CD player and heard the music of Beethoven, one of his dad's favorites. But when "Ode to Joy" came on, John switched it off. The irony of the song and the realities of his father's death was too much to contemplate.

He began unceremoniously packing the books into boxes the secretary had set out for him – research journals, references, and books for classes he had taught over the years – all the stuff that academics think they so desperately need to prove over and over again their status.

It was a game John had never wanted to play although he was certainly intelligent enough to be an academic if he had so chosen.

One curious item on his dad's desk was a tall statue of the UC Berkeley Campanile. John remembered that his dad had tried to get him to enroll at his alma mater. It seemed one of the few places for which his dad showed any sentimentality. Of course, John refused to apply and chose the opposite. The Navy proved to be a regimented lifestyle based on principle that fulfilled John's sense of self-pride. Like his dad, he was able to keep secrets, a skill he proved to himself time and again during top secret intelligence operations.

"Perhaps Joanie would like this statue," he thought worrying about his younger sister who now had a third tragedy to deal with in her short life. But as John reached over to pick up the slender statue to wrap it in newspaper, it slipped from his hand and cracked open as it hit the edge of the desk. Two rings fell out and bounced on the rug barely making a sound.

As John reached down to pick up the first one. He recognized the gold band with a single diamond that had always fit his mother's finger a bit loosely. As a very small child he liked to turn it round and round and round until she made him stop. He had never seen her take off that ring all the time he was growing up. John, attuned by years of training to be analytical, slowly twisted the ring. He surprised himself when tender memories of his mother swept over him. Looking more closely, he found an inscription on the inside of the ring that read, "To Rosa, All my love, Josh, Guadalajara, 1971." He didn't think that his father was that sentimental, but he presumed that he had loved his mother at one time. It perplexed him how a husband who apparently loves his wife can brutally murder her and hide the body. But from his own training, John knew that evil happened and he could only conjecture as to why. He was taught to see the signs of desperate people separating their emotional lives into compartments so that only their own survival matters. To look for "turning points" that pushed someone too far. Jealousy, hate or just normal circumstances, they can no longer control. They snap and feel forced to act in their own best interests. Although he was not as close to his father as the girls were, he thought he should have picked up these signals in his own father.

The other ring lay almost hidden in the green and golden brown area rug under his father's desk chair. The rug featured an impressionistic image of a deer with piercing doe eyes. "A dead deer," thought John sarcastically. "Professor Blagsdale would have liked that." He bent to pick up the ring and examined it in the lamplight. Another inscription read, "Por Juanita, cara mia, Josh, Venezuela, 1966. John put down the ring carefully. Who was Juanita? He had never heard his father mention that name and John prided himself on his indelible memory for detail. It was one of the skills that made him so valuable in his job. He knew he should call the police, but first he wanted to do a more thorough check of his father's office.

As John boxed the rest of the books on the first shelf, he skimmed the titles: psychology, sociology and Southwest archeology, and journals with research articles on the *favelas* of South America authored by his father. He noted how his father double stacked his books using the two-foot deep shelf most efficiently. Older books to the back, newer to the front – always the methodical mind. John found nothing, but he reasoned that if he did find something, it would be on the back of the shelf.

As he started in on the last shelf closest to his father's desk, John found a leather-bound journal hidden behind the second row of books. As he opened the pages, he saw his father's distinctive handwriting. He sat down in the swivel chair and began to read.

August 1960

My first days at Berkeley for Grad school... Strolled down Telegraph Avenue. This street is an education in itself. There are black-garbed beatniks left over from the 40s and 50s. They sit at outdoor cafes, strumming their guitars, tapping out rhythms on their bongo drums, and reading poetry to each other from Jack Kerouac??? Poetry is not my thing. I don't think they are university students, too old, too drugged – only hangers-on, not worth much.

60s hippies abound in colorful garb, and they are carrying textbooks on Marx and Lenin on their way past the hallowed Sather Gate. Never judge a weird book by its cover. These hippies could be some blooming geniuses like that pimply-faced 15-year-old I met in my advanced stats class. Around here you never know.

> *I bought this Italian leather journal from a sweet-looking gal at her open-air bookstall. I know I will never be a diarist; I tried that once as a teenager. Daily note-taking bores me! What I want to write is more than dates, weather and mundane activities. This journal will only hold my most important thoughts. So don't expect many entries.*

John ignored his dad's attempt at humor and skipped through some of the pages to 1962. In another section of the journal, John read several pages describing how his dad had defined his Ph.D. research problem and honed his reasoning about the methodology. He wrote that UC Berkeley was a prestigious university and no one would get through the process who was a slacker. He described the struggles he could foresee to defend his thesis before his Psychology Department committee. John thought it was one of the few times his dad seemed to doubt his own abilities. But further notes described each of his Ph.D. committee members and explained how he had figured out their academic mind games and how he would play his own hand accordingly in the next three years.

In a final entry in this section of the journal, his dad described his own research into the gang leaders from the black ghettos of Oakland and near-by Richmond. He briefly wrote of how these gang leaders jostled for position using an uneducated intelligence that sustained them through battles with rival gangs, police interrogations, and subsequent jailings. He wanted to know more about how the leaders became rich by manipulating their milieu, their women, their families and much of the socio-political systems in which they were entrapped. His dad called this character trait "hubris" and quoted the Webster dictionary definition: "a Greek term for arrogance caused by too great pride." His dad had questioned if this type of evil personality was genetic or a learned behavior, thinking perhaps it was only an adaptive instinct for survival.

In a self-reflective comment, Josh said he understood that he, a middle class, white male, shared some of these traits – a ruthlessness that helped one succeed against all odds. Josh underlined the next passage. "I will soon leave Berkeley to take up my post-doc position in Venezuela (finally a payback from my Ph.D. committee). I predict that there will be parallels with my California research findings. From what I have read, the lives of the young boys in the *favelas*, the shanty-town of Caracas, are not really so different from the kids in the ghettos of Oakland."

John paged forward to 1965. He was intrigued by one entry describing his dad's research on the leaders of the *favelas*. He even read it twice thinking it seemed to summarize his own father's psyche as he was beginning to understand him now.

> *By studying these boys who turn into super-human men, I realize that my own mindset sometimes has more in common with them than I choose to admit. Like them, no matter what, I will always choose to be a survivor.*

Other entries were sketchy, but then his father described meeting a beautiful Venezuelan girl. *"Juanita and I married 1966. Augostino Falls, Juanita had to fall. She was wearing those stiletto heels."* The entries were too cryptic to tell much else. A photo fell from between the pages and for the first time, John saw his father's first wife and he read the inscription on the back, "From your loving wife! Juanita, Caracas, 1968." He now realized that his mother, Rosa, was actually a second choice.

There were a few notes about meeting his mom and the birth of each of the kids. He seemed particularly proud when his first-born son arrived. John wished he could feel the same pride about his father. The man who had kept this journal seemed a complete stranger.

One odd entry concerned Paul Wilson, his dad's old friend, who got divorced and moved away when John was still young. He wrote, "Paul complimented me the other day by saying that he would have never had the courage to plan Sue's accident without me to act as an alibi." It was followed by one final line, "I didn't get my promotion, but Paul got his." John did not understand why such comments would rate space in this journal where so much else was left unwritten.

Then his father's writings became more and more verbose, almost obsessive. Five pages in cramped handwriting were written about Rosa's disappearances and how she was in over her head and yet admiration for her *valentía*, that stubborn courage of her convictions. This praise was followed by a sarcastically scathing remark about why Rosa's novel would get recognition before he got a better appointment. As John read the words, he could almost feel his father's hidden and increasing hostility, "The cartel dangers may prove useful to me in the end."

John read the next sentence, but it seemed out of context. *"That boy should not have been there."* This was followed by one of the quotes John found scattered throughout the journal. " *A man's character is his fate." Heraclites.* John couldn't figure out if these words were referring to the mysterious boy or to his father so he read on.

> *Everything else was planned. The boy should not have been at that gas station so late at night. Even the rain gods agreed and they erased my footsteps but not his presence. Rosa was my love, but she was too intelligent, she shouldn't have succeeded before me. It had to be.*

This entry was followed by one final quote: *"If what we do now is to make no difference in the end, then all the seriousness of life is done away with." Philosopher Ludwig Wittgenstein.* John had no idea what his father was ranting about, but there seemed to be a final desperation in his words.

There were great gaps of time in the journal. No daily life events, as his dad had promised at the beginning. No remorse at his mother's disappearance, and now John understood the reasons for her deliberately planned murder. No mention of how Julia and Joanie coped after her disappearance. Yet, John was surprised by one short entry about himself.

> *John is where he should be now. Maybe the*
> *Navy's code of honor will channel the genes*
> *he inherited from me in a positive way.*

John was not mentioned again, but then what else was new. His father had always acted a bit apprehensive around him even when he was a child, as if he were supposed to know something secret about his father. He realized, ironically, that the journal proved that he had never had even a clue about his father's real personality and that they had remained strangers to each other. John had always harbored gut-level suspicions about his mother's untimely disappearance, but because he was a young teenager and a worried son, the police just dismissed his concerns. Back then, after the initial investigation was closed, the police, convinced of Rosa Blagsdale's death by a Mexican cartel, had kept a "hands-off" policy regarding the highly respected professor and his family.

John tried to visualize the time elapsed since his mother's sudden disappearance – eight years. John knew this time was filled with his father meeting and living with Cheryl. But he had left for the Navy, Julia had left for New York, and Joanie was finally growing up. Were those family details too mundane and not worthy of a journal entry? He paged through the rest of the journal and could find little mention of Cheryl.

His eye caught a troubling entry that did concern Cheryl. John did not know her very well, but the girls liked her and he knew from Julia's emails and little cards from Joanie that this woman had truly cared for his sisters. Yet, his father wrote the last few entries in a hand that seemed even less steady.

> *I had to leave my beautiful Juanita behind because of "green-tape," so she couldn't*

come with me. My new job at Brandon couldn't wait. My Rosa, my rose, my children's beautiful mother, my great companion, shouldn't have blossomed so early. I should have been the one. It was distressing to have to pluck this flower so soon. The boy…that boy was just collateral damage, "cargo" as Rosa used to say. It's confirmed now. The new job will come through next August. This time, I cannot be burdened with someone lesser than myself. She would never fit in. The girls are grown now. Cheryl's suicide is inevitable.

John set the journal back on the orderly desk and bent down to pick up a large fragment of the campanile statue. How come only two rings fell out, where was Cheryl's? They weren't married, but Joanie wrote that his dad had given her a very nice emerald ring to mark their first five years. John shook out the broken statue, looking for a third ring but there wasn't one. He realized his suspicions were right. His father had only used Cheryl for his convenience and didn't care enough to leave a memento of her in this hidden place. John thought to himself that even Cheryl did not deserve the disrespectful death she had endured because of his father's selfish needs.

John picked up the journal again hoping to find some sense of guilt in his father's writing. Instead he read:

> *The flash flood was something I never counted on. Have the gods conspired against me at last? I will now have to carry out the ultimate act. I will drive to my favorite mountain spot above our cabin near Creekside. I will be hunting whatever prey is in season. The gun will go off accidentally -- getting caught on a willow branch. My death will be mourned by my sad, orphaned children, all my successful students over the years, and my academic friends and colleagues. Mine will have been a life of pride.*

John knew that the police delayed in arresting his father after his mother's body was found. The *Highlands Herald* reported that the county sheriff hadn't had time to interview the professor and they were supposedly following other leads, but John knew better. His mother had gone missing from the public library so the Highlands city police investigated. When they couldn't find the body, the New Mexico Bureau of Investigation was brought in to do a state-wide search. When Rosa's travels across state lines to Texas were revealed, they had to involve the FBI. And when clues pointed to her possible murder by an international cartel, OIA was brought in. The irony was that when her body washed out in Rio Seco County, the jurisdiction reverted to the county sheriff. John understood that too many political fingers had been in the pie for any one police entity to arrest his dad quickly.

John reflected with a bit of satisfaction that his dad did not have enough time for the carefully crafted exit he had envisioned in his journal. Instead, his father's life shattered around him too quickly, pressed by the police about Cheryl's death and the confirmation of Rosa's body. For once, his father's life was completely out of his control. John knew that Joanie had driven to the airport to pick up Julia, giving his dad only a small window of time to carry out his necessary suicide. Instead of the one final blaze of hubris Josh Blagsdale had hoped for, his self-inflicted death was viewed as the cowardly deed of a murderer.

As John closed his eyes and leaned back in his father's comfortable brown leather chair, his naval training took over. His mind tried to tie up all the loose ends. Who was this Juanita and the boy his father had mentioned? It was time to put in a few calls – to the local police first and later to his buddies in international intelligence who specialized in Mexico and Venezuela. Right now, he asked to speak to Detective Hildago, who was in charge of his mother's reopened case. "Detective, I have some new evidence I think you should see."

Saddened and angered, John waited for the officer. Up until this time, he had had no idea of his father's tainted past nor of his continuing deceit. To calm himself, John flipped through a magazine on his dad's desk, one with a yellow sticky note marked "research." This edition of *Newsweek* featured an article called "Overcoming Sin" by Kenneth L. Woodward. John read, "Ultimately, we become what we love. Hell is not a place, but a community of those who remain outside the circle of Divine

Embrace. All are called to enter heaven, but it is hubris to suppose that any one of us is worthy of a free ticket." Was it just coincidence that his dad was researching his own type of psychological personality? It seemed an incriminating type of article to have on your desk when you knew you had murdered someone. Perhaps the professor didn't believe it applied to him.

The article reiterated some of the terrorist concepts in his Afghanistan pre-op training manuals. John realized that, in his own way, his father was a personal terrorist, killing those who did not fit his grandiose life plan. Lovers, wives, and children – they seemed outwardly important at the time and maybe they even once held some value. But in the end, they each could be discarded at will. How could he and his sisters be the issue of such a man so filled with hubris? Could that character flaw surface in their own lives?

John felt an intuition that he was marked with the sin of his father.

Epilogue

It was Sunday morning. Sue Wilson sat reading her newspaper in the cozy room she had renovated two years before. Early fall sunlight streamed through the hanging geranium baskets, making slats of amber on the pale green wallpaper. Sue felt lucky to be alive. The vicious death of her friend Rosa and the exposed secrets of Josh's murders had rocked her so viscerally that she finally took the plunge and joined an AA group in town. She was surprised by some of the people there, even a couple from the university, but she had stuck it out for two years now. The kids were off to college and her mom called now and then. Basically Sue had salvaged her own life.

She sipped her coffee and browsed the headlines of the *Highlands Herald*:

Partisan battle erupts over possible release of

Clinton's videotaped testimony.

WASHINGTON (AllPolitics, September 15) -- A battle is brewing in the House Judiciary Committee as Republican and

Democratic members are at odds over releasing the videotaped version of President Bill Clinton's grand jury testimony. This latest bad news for the White House comes on the heels of tough criticism from two top Democratic leaders over the president's defense strategy.

More Lewinsky-Clinton scandal! In Sue's mind it didn't compare to the shock Josh Blagsdale had brought to their insular academic community.

Hurricane Season Passes its Prime

NASA -- Thunderstorm studies continue as a new hurricane candidate wends its way from Africa.

For once Sue was glad that she had chosen to stay in arid southwest New Mexico despite the suggestions of her mom and kids that she move back home near the Atlantic coast. Flipping through a few more pages, her eye caught a small article on the left inside column:

Lone Motorcyclist Killed on Dangerous Mountain Curve

John T. Blagsdale, 23, died in a single motorcycle accident on September 15th near Creekside. He was driving up Hwy 56 sometime after midnight, according to the coroner's office, when his motorcycle left the roadway on a curve. Sheriff Manuel Gonzales said the motorcycle skidded on the gravel embankment and was airborne for 22 feet before hitting the rock face on the side of the road. Blagsdale, home on leave from the Navy, was scheduled to rejoin his Special Intelligence Forces Unit in Afghanistan on Monday.

Funeral arrangements are pending.

www.ingramcontent.com/pod-product-compliance
Ingram Content Group UK Ltd.
Pitfield, Milton Keynes, MK11 3LW, UK
UKHW020141250726
13967UKWH00002B/798

9 781425 180744